More Answers

More Answers

by

Dorothy Martin

MOODY PRESS

CHICAGO

©1959, 1985 by
THE MOODY BIBLE INSTITUTE
OF CHICAGO
Revised Edition

Original title: *More Answers for Peggy*

Scripture quotations are from the
New King James Version.

ISBN: 0-8024-8303-8

1 2 3 4 5 6 7 Printing/LC/Year 90 89 88 87 86 85

Printed in the United States of America

1

Peggy stopped in the middle of the letter she was writing home and looked out the open window, feeling the warm evening breeze. The leaves on the tree outside the window rustled and gave her a sense of peace she had never expected to experience in this house. She had left her bedroom door partly open and, by turning slightly in her desk chair, she could see Jane sprawled on her bed, leafing through a magazine, while her stereo was at a volume Aunt Emily approved of.

Peggy reread what she had written so far.

"I still can't get used to the idea that it's warm here all year round. I thought I wouldn't miss the cold and snow, but I do—sort of. Jane and I are going to do some final Christmas shopping tomorrow. I'm glad I bought for all of you early, and I hope you will like what I got you. You'll see what I got for Bill when he opens it. You three were easy to buy for, and I even got something for Alice and for Ann without too much trouble. But Jane is the problem—I don't have the faintest idea what to buy her."

She stopped writing and doodled swirls around the margin of the paper. Much as she wanted to, she couldn't let on how desperately she had hoped she could go home for Christmas. Bill was only a few hours away from home by bus. But a trip home for Peggy was impossible. California was too far from Pennsylvania, and the trip too expensive for the little time she could be home.

5

She had hoped that Aunt Emily would see how much she longed to go and give her the money as a Christmas present. She could so easily. The money would mean nothing to her. But as though she could read her mind, Aunt Emily had said last week, "It's just as well you are not going home for a visit, Peggy. You would only have to come back for the rest of the year, so there is no need to get yourself all unsettled. It won't be long until you will be going home for good."

Peggy had thought if she could just go home for a week she wouldn't mind coming back again. It was like refusing a starving man one meal because it might make him want another. But she had learned to argue with Aunt Emily silently. So she had only said aloud, "I suppose so," knowing the longing was clear in her voice.

She gnawed her pen for a moment and then went on. "They really go in for Christmas in a big way here. They've got the most beautiful decorations you ever saw all over the house and two big Christmas trees. One is in the living room and is absolutely *gorgeous* now that it's all decorated. The other one is in the breakfast room in front of the French doors, and that's beautifully decorated too. I guess that one is really for the help. At least I saw some presents under it for them."

Peggy stopped here as she realized how casually she had used the word *help*. Just six months ago when she had come for what was supposed to be only a summer visit, the idea of servants had been so strange to her that she had felt apologetic whenever one of them did something for her. Now she took it as a matter of course. *Don't you ever, ever get snobbish the way Aunt Emily is,* she scolded herself fiercely.

She forced her thoughts back to the letter. "Thanks for the extra money you sent for presents. I can really use it. I wish I knew what to get for Uncle Walter. He's already got everything. I saw a really beautiful white scarf that I'll get Aunt Emily. I don't know if she'll ever use it, but it's so pretty. It's really just a soft cloud of material. I found a clever pattern for aprons in a magazine one day so I made one each for the cook and both maids. They're real cute and sort of unusual. That helped a little because the material didn't cost very much so I've got some extra. Money, I mean. But I've *still* got to think of something for Jane."

She stopped as Jane asked from the doorway, "What're you doing?"

"Writing a letter home. Come in. I'm almost through."

Jane flopped on the bed, then got up and picked up a sheet of paper from the desk.

"What's this?"

"Oh, just sketches of doll dresses I might make for a little kid I baby-sit at home."

Peggy hastily finished and stuck the letter in an envelope.

"It's funny to think we didn't know each other until last Christmas. Just one year ago." Jane stared down at the sketches.

Peggy nodded but couldn't help thinking they still didn't know each other very well now—at least not the way sisters should.

She cupped her chin in her hand and looked at Jane thoughtfully. "I sometimes wonder how things would have been if Mother and Dad had been able to keep us all together when we were little instead of your coming out here to live with Aunt Emily and Uncle Walter."

"I wouldn't have liked it." Jane's voice was flat, positive.

"You don't really know. You think that now because that's the way things turned out. But if they'd been different—"

"I'm glad they weren't. What do you want to imagine

7

dumb things like that for?" Jane's voice was angry now, but at the same time she sounded upset. "I wouldn't want things to be any different than they are!"

Peggy was sure Jane was thinking only of how she would hate not having the beautiful things her aunt and uncle had given her. And of course they were parents to her, while Mother and Dad were really strangers.

But she went on stubbornly. "I think it would have been fun if we'd grown up together. Especially now that we're older. With you in sixth and Bill in seventh and me in eighth, we could do lots of things together." Then Peggy said something she knew she wouldn't have dared say to Jane three months before. "I guess God puts people in the places they're supposed to be."

Jane really sounded angry as she demanded, "Why do you have to say things like that?"

"Because it's what I think."

"Well, I wish you wouldn't. Especially around other kids. They'll think you're funny or something."

"I don't talk about God very much. Not as much as I should," Peggy admitted honestly.

"We just don't—I mean, the kids I go around with don't talk about God at all."

"They go to church—some of them."

"Well, of course, but that's different. That's something you do, but you don't talk about it all the time. You're not supposed to."

"We really should though, Jane," Peggy began. "Everyone who is a Christian is supposed to—"

"Honestly, Peggy, you make me so mad sometimes! You sound as though you're the only one who knows anything about things like that. I wish you'd quit talking about it." Jane got up and stormed out of the room.

Peggy looked after her, half angry and yet glad that Jane's usual indifference had been shattered. She thought of how hard she had tried to become friends with Jane and knew she had made some progress. At first she hadn't cared, thinking she would be visiting only three months. Then had come the word that a whole year stretched ahead of her.

As she began to get ready for bed, she thought back to the many tears of homesickness she had cried when she first knew she would have to spend the school year in her aunt's home. Gradually she realized her parents needed the year to work out their personal problems and get her father safely established in a teaching career. She had made herself accept the fact that she must stay in California while Bill stayed with Uncle Ed on the farm. She had sensed also that the year would give an opportunity to let Jane and Aunt Emily and Uncle Walter know she was a Christian.

And it really hadn't been so bad. It was Christmas already, and the months ahead until she could go home did not seem so interminable after all. In fact they would hardly give time enough to make any change in Jane the way things were going now. They had got to the place where they could be together and talk about things and, to some extent, share ideas. But that was all.

Peggy sighed. If it weren't for Lisa—here the sigh turned into a smile. She had seen Lisa only two times since that day in August when Lisa had accepted the Lord Jesus as her Savior. Aunt Emily had reluctantly allowed the visits when Lisa had come to help her mother do the laundry. Peggy sobered as she thought again of the brief glimpse she had had of Lisa's home life. She knew Mrs. Vanacek worked constantly for her aunt and other people, but thought she did it just to help out her husband's salary. But Lisa on the second visit had said simply, "My father drinks."

"Oh," Peggy had replied. Then because Lisa looked

so miserable she had said,"Well, so does Uncle Walter—and even my aunt a little."

But Lisa had only shaken her head and answered, "Not the way my father does. He does it all the time. That's why my mother works. So we can eat."

Then Lisa had said confidently, "But someday he won't. Someday he will listen to someone explain how he can be set free, and then he'll be saved."

And Peggy had found herself swallowing a lump in her throat while a feeling of shame swept over her. And *she'd* been grousing about having to live with Aunt Emily.

She frowned now as she came back to the immediate problem that faced her. What could she get Jane for a present? It would be simple if only Jane liked to read. "If I could get her a book and maybe something else—"

She put down her hairbrush as a sudden and exciting thought came. *Maybe I could get her a Bible. She's only got that small New Testament with real small print.* She frowned at herself in the mirror and shrugged the thought away. *I guess that would be a waste of money. She wouldn't like it.*

But the idea returned again and again the next day as she and Jane went shopping with Miss Murphy. She found the scarf for Aunt Emily and finally settled on a tie for Uncle Walter, though she hated getting him something so ordinary. Pushing away the idea of a Bible, she bought a set of different colored bracelets that would match several of Jane's sweaters.

"If you girls can find something to do now for a while, I've got to take care of some business for your aunt before we go home," Miss Murphy said after lunch in the store tearoom.

"How long will you be?" Jane asked.

"Oh, an hour at least, probably closer to two."

"Let's go to a movie," Jane suggested. "I've done that other times when I've had to wait for you."

"There wouldn't be time enough," Peggy began slowly, but Miss Murphy broke in.

"That's a good idea. I won't have to feel rushed if I know you are occupied. Come along. The theater down the street has something playing. I noticed it as we came from the parking lot. It's not a Disney film, but it has a PG rating so it should be all right."

She started off briskly with Jane while Peggy lagged behind, trying to think of some reason to get out of going. She thought of the things she knew Jane watched on TV. Some of them were programs that Mr. Parker said were like mud that left dirt on your hand—except that the programs left dirt in your mind. She had never been brave enough to say that to Jane. And now this movie looked like some of the TV shows.

What possible excuse could she give Jane for not going? To say she didn't want to go because she was a Christian sounded too goody-goody. And anyway, Jane wouldn't understand that.

Helplessly she followed them down the escalator, through the revolving doors of the store, and joined the crowds that jammed the streets for last-minute shopping. Then she was walking behind Jane down the aisle of the darkened theater with Miss Murphy's reminder ringing in her ears, "I'll pick you up here after you've seen it once. Wait right in front."

Just this once won't matter, she argued with herself as she looked up at the screen without even seeing what was playing. *I wouldn't do it at home, of course, but there's not much I can do about it if Jane wants to see this.*

But she knew she was being cowardly, afraid of Jane's scorn. *I can't leave now,* she argued with herself. *Miss Murphy will expect to find us here when she comes back. Besides, I shouldn't leave Jane here alone.* She settled back to watch and listen.

She shifted uncomfortably at the first swear words from the pretty high school girl who was the center of the story. Then, as other scenes became more explicit, she wanted to put her hand over Jane's eyes and say, "Don't look."

Laughter washed around them as an athletic young surfer held an old man's head under water until he seemed to be drowning. Peggy glanced at Jane, who was listening intently though she wasn't laughing.

"Jane. Do you think we should go?"

"Of course not. It's not over."

"I don't think it's very funny."

"I don't either, but it's good."

Peggy stared up at the screen, alive with figures saying and doing things that were wrong. Remembered words beat against her mind. "Whatever things are good—pure—lovely ... think about those things." There was nothing here like that. She would have to get out. Jane had done this before while Miss Murphy was busy. She would be all right alone.

She leaned over to Jane and whispered, "There's something I want to buy. I'll go back and get it now. You can stay if you want to."

"But Miss Murphy will wait while you get it afterward," Jane whispered back.

"I'll hurry and come back in time," Peggy replied. "I'll watch the time and meet you out in front."

Without waiting for a reply, she slipped out of her seat and practically ran up the aisle. Outside she looked around to locate the direction of the store and then hurried along the street and in through the door. Remembering that Miss Murphy had consulted the directory just inside the front entrance for the floor she wanted, she did the same and then took the elevator to the book section on the seventh floor. She looked around at the bright-colored book jackets as she walked past the counters.

"May I help you?"

"Yes, I'd like to see the Bibles."

"Over here on this counter. What kind do you want?"

"I don't know exactly."

"Is it for a relative?"

"Yes."

"Then you'll probably want something with large print. We have this kind." The clerk laid a big Bible down on the counter.

"That's awfully big," said Peggy doubtfully.

"It has to be big for the print to be large enough to read. We have some New Testaments with the same large print. Would you like to see one?"

"No, she has a New Testament. But don't you have the whole Bible in a smaller size?"

"Not with large print," the clerk replied a little impatiently.

"That doesn't matter."

"Usually older people have trouble reading fine print."

"This isn't for someone older."

"I thought you wanted it for a relative."

"I do. My sister, But she's eleven."

"Oh!" The clerk eyed Peggy with surprise and doubt. As she laid out several sizes of Bibles, she said, "Have you seen the other books we have? I mean, Bibles are all right, of course, but we have several special books on sale during the Christmas season that would be just right for an eleven-year-old."

"No, this is what I want. How much is it?"

"Fifteen dollars."

"Fifteen dollars! Do you have anything—I mean, aren't there any that cost a little less?"

"Yes, this one is ten dollars; here's one for six."

There was no doubt that the fifteen-dollar one was the best, but Peggy knew without looking in her purse that she didn't have nearly that much money left. If only she had bought this first instead of the other stuff! *Maybe I can exchange the other gift,* she thought hopefully. Then her shoulders sagged. The other packages were in the car. Miss Murphy had taken them so they wouldn't have to hang onto them during the movie.

I can't ask her to wait while I exchange Jane's other gift and get this, Peggy thought. *Maybe I'll have to let it go after all.*

She could tell the clerk was tired of waiting for her to make up her mind and began reluctantly to shake her head. But as she did, an unwelcome thought pushed its way into her mind as she remembered Lisa's gift lying snugly in her bag.

No, I can't do that! she protested inwardly. *I bought that necklace just especially for her. I'm sure she's never had anything as pretty as this.*

She hadn't really intended to spend so much for Lisa's gift, but when she saw the dainty necklace, it reminded her so much of Lisa that she had impulsively bought it. Since the package was so tiny, she had slipped it into her bag so it wouldn't be lost.

She looked again at the Bibles and picked up the six-dollar one. There was no concordance in the back and no maps. And it didn't have a very nice cover.

Not that it will make any difference to Jane, she argued with herself. *She probably won't use it enough to amount to fifteen dollars. If there were just some other way I could do it—*

But there wasn't. And she would have to hurry to get back in time to meet Miss Murphy.

"I'll be right back," she said to the clerk, who was drumming her fingers impatiently on the counter. "I want the fifteen-dollar one, but I have to do something else first."

Hurrying down to the first floor, she went over to the jewelry counter where she had bought Lisa's necklace and waited until the woman who had originally waited on her was free. The clerk was reluctant to make the exchange at first but finally talked to a supervisor who approved it. Peggy picked out a cheaper necklace, not nearly as pretty, and rushed back up to the seventh floor.

If Lisa knew, she'd be happy, she reminded herself.

But she found it hard not to regret the sacrifice she had caused Lisa when Jane complained all the way home because she had been left alone.

Maybe it will be worth it someday, she thought, and tried to ignore Jane's complaints and curious questions about where she had gone.

2

Because Aunt Emily didn't like to make any change in their customary pattern of life even for Christmas, she decided they would open their gifts Christmas Eve before she and Uncle Walter left for a late dinner engagement.

Peggy stood by the window in the living room where she could see the tree reflected in front of her as well as in the mirror on the wall behind her. Aunt Emily's packages were so beautifully wrapped that Peggy almost hated to open them and spoil their appearance.

It's just like her to have everything done to perfection, Peggy thought. But then anyone could be like that who only had to tell someone else what to do. It had been Miss Murphy who had done the shopping, on Aunt Emily's instructions of course, and she had wrapped the gifts.

*But Jane's packages look the same way, while mine—*Peggy turned and looked at the presents she had just slipped under the tree. To her they looked knobby and the ribbons skimpy. She got a scared feeling as she caught sight of her gift to Jane and impulsively reached down to take out the package that was the Bible. Jane wouldn't like it at all, and there was no telling what Aunt Emily would say about it. But before she could reach it, the door opened and Jane came in with Uncle Walter. He sat down in an easy chair; Jane sat beside him on the floor.

"Well, Peggy." Her uncle cleared his throat as he nodded at her. "You like the tree?"

"Oh, yes, it's beautiful!"

It was. Every one of the delicate ornaments was placed in just the right relation to the next so there were no bare spots. The tinsel hung evenly, and the lights glowed just as though the distance between each had been carefully measured. That was practically what had happened. Peggy knew because Aunt Emily had hired professional decorators to come in and do the trees and decide on what decorations should be used throughout the house.

The tree looks more beautiful decorated, but it doesn't seem as though it belongs to us when it's that way, she thought. But she knew her aunt would never allow anything to be done in her house unless it was done perfectly. Even to decorating a Christmas tree. She smiled as she thought of some of the lumpy things she and Bill had made in school when they were younger and had brought home, confidently expecting to put them on the front branches of the tree. She remembered that her mother had never been overly enthusiastic. It had been Dad who admired them extravagantly and helped fasten them on the tree.

I suppose Mother would be just like Aunt Emily in lots of ways if she could afford to be, Peggy thought with a trace of unease.

She turned as her aunt came into the living room, dressed for dinner. "We had better begin," Aunt Emily said as she came toward them quickly. "We must leave in an hour." She turned toward Jane. "Do you want to hand out the gifts?"

"OK. I'm dying to know what's in this one." Jane reached under the tree as she spoke and pulled out a big box addressed to her. She lifted it, shook it a little, and then regretfully laid it down and reached for one with her aunt's name on it.

Peggy couldn't believe the number of presents she received. At home she and Bill usually got one big thing from their parents—something they *needed*—and then some smaller gifts. Now the scarf she had bought for her aunt seemed awfully little in comparison to what Aunt Emily gave her. Most of the packages had sweaters and skirts and slacks.

"Thank you ever so much," she stammered finally, and her aunt replied, "I felt you needed them."

Peggy had forgotten to watch as Jane opened her gifts, engrossed as she was in her own. She looked up just in time to see her tear off the wrapping from the Bible and stare down at it.

Then she looked over at Peggy and said, "Thanks," and laid it down.

Aunt Emily looked at it and then at Peggy. "It's too bad you didn't know she already had a Bible. If you'd like we can have Miss Murphy exchange it." She looked at Jane as she spoke, but Peggy knew she was really talking to her.

All Jane said was, "Maybe," and reached for another package.

Peggy felt her face get hot. She'd known Aunt Emily wouldn't approve. In fact, she had really expected her to be angry. It wasn't so much *what* she said but the way she said things that made them sound so awful. *She seems to know just how to say the thing that makes what you think is important and wonderful seem so insignificant,* she thought resentfully. *Just like now.*

What little pleasure Peggy had anticipated in a family Christmas was lost now, and she was glad when Aunt Emily rose, followed by Uncle Walter, and smiled down at the girls as they sat on the floor surrounded by their gifts.

"We must leave now, but I'm sure you don't need us to help you entertain yourselves. Thank you both for your gifts to us. Peggy, I think your scarf will fit well with what I plan to wear this evening. The weather is a little cool, and this will go nicely with my dinner dress."

Peggy's face flushed with pleasure. It was *so* nice to have done something that really pleased Aunt Emily.

At first neither one spoke after their aunt and uncle had left until Peggy said finally, "Thanks a lot for all the things you gave me. But you spent more on me than I did on you."

Jane only shrugged.

"I've already read these books, but I've always wanted to own them." Peggy rubbed her hand over the bindings. Then she looked over at her sister, hardly believing she had heard correctly as Jane said, "I like what you gave me too."

"Do you really?" She was sure Jane was referring to the Bible and not the bracelets. "I was scared you wouldn't."

"You scared?" Jane's voice carried such a note of disbelief that Peggy stared back at her. "I didn't think you were scared of anything."

Peggy knew her mouth was hanging open, and she shut it, feeling in a state of shock. "You think I'm not afraid of anything?" She heard her voice climb in a squeak of surprise, but she couldn't seem to control it.

"Well, you act as though you know everything—"

"I don't either!"

"You think everyone should believe the same things you do. And not everyone does." Jane's voice carried a challenge that Peggy heard and knew she should answer. But she couldn't make herself say the words. She felt her mind scrambling for the kind of things Bill could say so easily.

Why couldn't she say with a confident smile that it wasn't what *she* believed that made something right? That a person had to believe what God said in the Bible. And the only way to know what He said was to read it.

And why couldn't she just say, "Jane, why don't we decide we'll both read the same verses every day?"

But she felt as though her throat were closed and no words could get through. And then her chance was gone because Jane started picking up her presents, stacking them in a heap to carry up to her room. It was clear she didn't want to talk anymore, and Peggy was glad.

As Peggy began sorting her presents, the door opened and a maid came in with a tray of hot chocolate and tiny, decorated cakes. She put the tray down on a table beside the fireplace and handed Peggy a small package.

"This was left for you under the tree in the breakfast room."

"Thank you." Peggy looked at the card without recognizing the writing. She tore open the envelope and glanced quickly at the short note.

Dear Peggy,
     This isn't very much and maybe you'll get another one. If you do, I'll exchange this. If not, I thought you'd like to keep a diary. I always do. And now that I'm saved, it's even more fun because there's so much more to write about. This Christmas means so much more to me than any did before. I can't thank you enough for helping me find the real meaning of Christmas.
                                   Love, Lisa

"What is it? Who's it from?"

"It's a diary." She yanked off the white tissue paper. "From Lisa. Isn't it nice? I had one in fifth grade, but I didn't write in it very much."

"I've got one too, but I always forget to put anything

21

in for the day until I'm in bed, and then I don't want to bother to get out."

"That's the way I was." Peggy looked down at the diary and said with emphasis, "But this time I'm going to write in it every night."

"I suppose because *she* gave it to you."

Peggy looked at Jane, surprised at the oddly jealous tone of her voice. "Well, yes, partly," she answered defiantly. "What's wrong with that?"

Jane shrugged. "I hope you don't think I care anything about *her*."

"Honestly, you make me so—" Peggy stopped. Jane's snobbishness, like Aunt Emily's, never failed to make her boil with anger. She turned and picked up a cup of chocolate and held it out to Jane. She made herself smile at her as she explained seriously, "You see, I know Lisa can't afford very much, and I think it was awfully nice of her to give me something when she has other people to buy things for."

"You like her present more than you do mine," Jane sulked. "And mine cost more. And, besides, you should like mine better because I'm your sister."

"I like the books very much," Peggy protested. She was tempted to remind Jane that she was the one who preferred people to think she and Peggy were cousins instead of sisters, but decided not to.

"In some ways I sort of think of Lisa as a sister too."

Jane turned toward the door. Over her shoulder she said coldly, "I don't think I care for your old Bible after all."

"You should!" Peggy flashed back. "It might do you some good if you'd read it!"

She regretted the words the minute they were out of her mouth. But it was too late to recall them because Jane burst from the room and ran up the stairs. Peggy ran after her calling, "Wait, Jane! I'm sorry! I didn't mean what I said!"

But a slammed bedroom door was Jane's only reply, and Peggy sighed. The evening had gone so well, and then she had messed it up.

3

She began using her diary by writing down the day's events before going to bed that night. The entry the next night was written in bitter words. She had asked her aunt's permission to see Lisa when she came to help with the extra holiday laundry. Aunt Emily had refused.

"Peggy, when this matter was discussed before, we reached an agreement. I intend to abide by it, and I intend that you shall also."

"But this is different," Peggy argued. "I only want to see her long enough to thank her for her present." She looked at her aunt and knew from the expression on her face that it was hopeless. But she plunged ahead anyway. "She hasn't very much money, and she has other people to buy things for, and it wouldn't be very nice of me if I didn't even thank her."

"You may write a note and give it to one of the maids to take down. That will be sufficient."

"But, Aunt Emily—"

Her aunt held up her hand. "Now, Peggy, please do not argue. I've made my position clear to you regarding the status of the people who work in this house. I will not hear anything from you on the matter—now or in the future."

It was useless to protest longer, so Peggy bit her lip to hold back the angry words. But she poured out her feelings that evening in her diary.

It just wasn't fair of Aunt Emily to condemn Lisa when she didn't know her at all. Just because she was poor didn't mean she wasn't as good as other people. But that's what Aunt Emily thought, and Jane did too. Lisa could never be inferior to anyone. She was beautiful and smart and nice. Even Aunt Emily would see that if she would let herself.

She sighed and reached for a piece of paper. She might as well give up the idea of seeing Lisa and get a note written. But somehow she couldn't seem to get started because she didn't know what to say without hurting Lisa's feelings. Finally she gave up, thinking there would be time to do it later.

Then she forgot about it the next day and wasn't reminded of it until the day after that when the maid said as she served lunch, "That girl is downstairs and asked if you were here."

"Oh, I forgot she would be here today."

"She sure is a beauty."

"What'll I do?"

"Why? What's the matter? Don't you want to see her?"

"Yes, but—"

"Scared of her mother?"

"No, but I'm not supposed to—I mean, my aunt—" Peggy stopped, embarrassed, but the maid nodded understandingly. "Sure, I know. You're too good to talk to the hired help."

"Please! I don't think that!"

"Some people in this house do." The maid's voice was angry. Then she said, "You don't have to go down. I'll tell her you can't."

"Oh, but I want to. And I don't want her to know my aunt feels that way."

The maid gave a short laugh. "Nobody has to *tell* her

26

that. She can feel it the minute she steps onto the grounds."

"If she could only come up to my room," Peggy said wistfully. "But she won't and anyway—" Peggy stopped abruptly. She had meant to say, "My aunt would have a fit," but she didn't want to be disloyal.

"I've got an idea. Why not go down to the recreation room?" the maid suggested.

"But how will that help?"

"Well, if you just *happen* to be there and what's-her-name just *happens* to come out and start talking, it isn't your fault, is it?"

In her heart Peggy knew it would be, and that she would be deliberately disobeying her aunt. But because she wanted so much to see Lisa and because she didn't think it was right for Aunt Emily to make such an unfair rule, she nodded.

"I could do that just this once. Then I can tell Lisa I can't see her anymore."

"Sure, and your aunt won't know the difference. *I'll* never tell."

Peggy hurried with her lunch, thankful that Jane was visiting Stella and wasn't home to complicate things. Aunt Emily would never go down to the basement. Even so, she looked around furtively as she ran quickly and silently up to her room to see if Aunt Emily might possibly be upstairs. No one was in sight as she sped along the thickly carpeted hall to the back of the house and ran quietly down to the basement. She hurried over to the laundry room door and pushed it open. Mrs. Vanacek turned from the ironing board and gave her a grudging smile.

"We were wondering if you'd be down." Then raising her voice sharply, "Lisa! Here she is."

Lisa appeared in the doorway from the room where she had been putting clothes into the dryer.

"Hi."

'Hi." Peggy smiled at her and then, glancing nervously over her shoulder, half-expecting to see her aunt suddenly appear, she added "Can you come out in the rec room for a little while?"

Lisa looked inquiringly at her mother, who nodded but said, "Only a little while. There's a lot of work to do, and you can't just sit around and gab." Lisa gave her mother a loving squeeze as she passed her, which Peggy could tell both pleased and embarrassed Mrs. Vanacek.

"I can't stay down very long anyway," she said as they crossed the room to a sofa.

"How are you?" Lisa asked shyly. "I haven't had a chance to see you lately when I've come to help my mother."

"I know. But I've thought a lot about you. I'd like to come and talk more but my aunt—" She stopped, struggling for the right words that would explain the situation.

But Lisa looked away, rubbing her hand over the frayed seam of her jeans. "I know. It's all right." Then changing the subject abruptly she said, "I've had some letters from Ann Parker. I was so surprised to get the first one because I couldn't think of anyone I knew in Pennsylvania. But she explained right away that her dad is the minister of the church where you go at home and that you had written her about me. She sounds like a wonderful person."

"She is!" Peggy exclaimed fervently. "I wish you could meet her sometime."

"Well, I guess I will in heaven," Lisa answered simply.

Peggy looked at her wistfully, thinking, *I wouldn't have thought to say that,* and was reminded again how much alike Lisa and Bill were. They both seemed to find it so easy to believe and so easy to talk about what they believed. They did it as naturally as though they were talking about the weather or their favorite food. *Why* couldn't she have done that with Jane the other evening?

"She told me all about everyone in your church," Lisa was saying. "About your brother and Tom and Lois and Daniel."

"She must have written lots of letters."

"I think about three or four. I feel as though I know her better than the kids I grew up with." She paused thoughtfully. "I suppose it's because since I've been saved I don't see things the way I used to. I even feel closer to you, when I hardly know you, than I do to my old friends."

She smiled at Peggy and then jumped up. "I'd better go back and help Mother. And thanks for the necklace. I've never had anything so pretty. I'm going to wear it next week for a special program we're having at school."

"What are you going to do?"

"I have to give an original speech, and I'm kind of scared. Maybe the necklace will boost my morale a little."

"I'd love to hear you!" Peggy exclaimed impulsively.

"Would you? Do you think you could come?"

Peggy shook her head regretfully. "I guess I can't. Someone would have to take me, and I know my aunt would not let me go."

"I wish I could say we'd come and get you, but my dad—" Lisa stopped for a moment and then finished in a low voice. "My dad might not be able to go himself, and I wouldn't want to promise that he'd come for you and then not have him show up."

Peggy hoped the relief she felt didn't show in her face. She could just imagine what Aunt Emily would say if she should announce she was going someplace with the Vanaceks!

"What are you going to wear?"

"I'm not sure yet exactly." Lisa's voice sounded slightly embarrassed, and Peggy was sorry she had asked.

Then her mind flashed to the new outfit she had just received from her aunt for a Christmas gift. She looked at Lisa, trying to imagine how it would look on her. It would be perfect.

"I've got just the thing," she exclaimed excitedly. "It's a skirt and blouse combination. The top is sort of like a sweater too and blouses over the skirt. It's burnt orange and amber—"

"Oh, thanks, Peggy, but I couldn't borrow it," Lisa interrupted.

"Why not?"

"Just because."

"Sure you can."

"It wouldn't be right to wear your clothes and pretend they were mine."

"You wouldn't be pretending," Peggy protested. "Jane and Stella trade clothes all the time. And Alice and I did too when I was home."

"That's different. This wouldn't be trading because you wouldn't be wearing anything of mine."

"I might sometime."

Lisa shook her head. "Besides, my mother wouldn't want me to do it."

"Do what?" The question came from the doorway, and the girls looked around at Mrs. Vanacek.

"What are you talking about, Lisa?" she demanded again, and Lisa looked unhappily away from the questioning frown on her mother's face.

"It's really nothing, Mother," she protested. "I was just telling Peggy about the program Monday, and she asked what I was going to wear."

"And I wanted her to wear something new I have that

would look just super on her," Peggy broke in, expecting Mrs. Vanacek's temper to explode at the idea of accepting charity from someone.

But when Lisa said, "I told her I didn't need it," her mother only looked at her thoughtfully and then back at Peggy.

"Why did you offer it?" she demanded.

"Because it would look super on her. And because I know what it's like to have to wear something old when everyone else is wearing something really sharp."

For a few minutes she was afraid she had said the wrong thing as Mrs. Vanacek frowned at her. Lisa nervously pulled at a thread in her jeans and waited for the explosion.

She looked up in amazement when she heard her mother say in a quiet voice, "I will let Lisa borrow the outfit if your aunt is willing for you to loan it."

Peggy gulped in dismay. Aunt Emily would never allow it. Never!

"I thought I would just—I mean I wasn't going to—" She stopped, almost in tears.

"You weren't going to tell her?"

"Well, they're my clothes," she replied defensively.

Neither of them answered, and Peggy added, "Jane always loans Stella things without asking."

"This is different." Mrs. Vanacek's voice was still quiet but anger was building up in it.

"No, it isn't," Peggy argued. But she knew Aunt Emily wouldn't agree with her. If Lisa's father were wealthy and able to buy her all the clothes she wanted, Aunt Emily would be glad to let Peggy loan her something. But here Lisa *needed* to borrow something, and her aunt would consider it improper to loan it.

"You ask your aunt," Mrs. Vanacek repeated obstinately. "Tell her you want Lisa to wear it and that it was

31

your idea. If she says yes, then it's OK with me. But she won't," she added positively and turned back into the laundry.

Lisa squeezed Peggy's hand tightly. "Thanks, Peggy. It was nice of you to think of it. But really it isn't necessary."

"I'm going to ask my aunt," Peggy replied stubbornly.

"No, please don't," Lisa begged. "It might make her think I had asked you for it, and then she might blame my mother and not let her come here to work, and we really need the money. And anyway, wearing the necklace you gave me, I'll feel dressed up even in my old clothes."

She smiled good-bye as she went back to the laundry room, and Peggy started slowly up the stairs. The mixture of emotions inside her began to sort themselves out as she reached her room without being seen.

The strongest emotion was a feeling of guilt. She had deliberately—no matter what anybody might say—deliberately disobeyed her aunt in going down to see Lisa. But she also felt almost weak with relief that her offer of the clothes had not been accepted. Aunt Emily might have found out somehow. Along with the relief was a nagging sense of shame that Mrs. Vanacek had had to do what she, as a Christian, should have done instinctively—be honest with her aunt. She had offered the clothes behind Aunt Emily's back, and Mrs. Vanacek had refused them unless Lisa could accept them openly.

Will I ever learn? she wondered in despair. *I never seem to make any progress in living like a Christian. I wasn't even supposed to go down there in the first place, even though no one will ever know.*

She frowned accusingly at herself in the mirror. "You ought to tell her," she said sternly. But her mirrored image shook her head obstinately. "I ought to, but I *can't!*"

4

It didn't help matters any to have Jane come home that evening wearing something entirely different from what she had worn when she had left in the morning.

"Stella and I traded," she answered casually when Peggy said, "I didn't know you had a skirt like that."

That evening, for almost the first time since she had found she would be staying here for the school year and had determined to make the best of it, Peggy let herself think longingly of home. How much easier it would be if she could only go home, right now, tonight. No Aunt Emily to cope with, no Jane to argue with, no Uncle Walter to feel responsible for—here she stopped. The thing was she *was* responsible for him, and going home would not make her less so. She was responsible for Jane, too, and for Aunt Emily, hard as that was.

She thought back to that day last August when she had won what had been the biggest battle of her Christian experience—being willing to stay on for the year and trust God to help her. But the doors that she had thought then were opening so readily to her slightest touch now seemed bolted shut, and no amount of pushing or knocking or pleading for admittance made any difference. She couldn't seem to do anything that would be a witness to anybody in the house. Even the maid now would think she was dishonest.

The trouble was it was so hard to *say* anything. She

just couldn't go up to Uncle Walter and tell him he wasn't a Christian. He wouldn't know what she was talking about, and Aunt Emily would turn icy. And as far as *living* like a Christian was concerned, she never saw Uncle Walter except at the dinner table. Her thoughts stopped abruptly, as she remembered her disobedience of that day.

She sighed. "I guess I might as well go and tell her, or I'll never feel right about it. It's such a little thing, and I'm probably crazy to own up. But she might find out about it somehow, and then I would be in trouble."

She got up from her curled-up position on the bed, combed her hair carefully, and made sure her blouse was tucked neatly in her slacks. Aunt Emily might forgive a lie but never sloppy appearance.

She went slowly down the wide stairs, the sound of her feet smothered in the thick carpeting, and hung over the bannister, listening for the sound of voices. She didn't know if there were guests or not and didn't want to barge in. Everything was quiet so she tiptoed on down, crossed the wide hall, and stood hesitating in the door of the living room. Uncle Walter was in a deep chair beside the fireplace, immersed in the paper. Aunt Emily sat across the room reading. She looked over at Peggy. "Well?"

Uncle Walter looked up too, and Peggy found her lips dry as she searched frantically for something to say on the spur of the moment. It was impossible to say anything to her aunt in front of Uncle Walter. But they were both looking at her expectantly, so she said the first thing that came into her mind.

"I—I just thought I would come down here for a while. It's kind of lonesome in my room." The excuse sounded impossible even to her. Why would she want their company? Or, even more unlikely, why would they want to visit with her?

"Just as you like," her aunt answered and went back to her book.

Uncle Walter returned to the newspaper without any comment at all. Peggy sat down on a low stool and stared at the fire which flickered lazily as though it realized it was completely unnecessary on such a mild evening. She stole a glance now and then at her uncle, wishing she had enough courage to begin a conversation with him. But what in the world could she find to talk about?

"Do you like to play checkers, Uncle Walter?" She could hardly believe it was her voice squeaking the question.

He looked at her, startled. "Checkers? No!" he said and went back to his paper.

"What *is* the matter, Peggy?" her aunt asked. "Can't you and Jane find something to do?"

Peggy stood up, defeated. "Yes, I guess so. I just thought I'd come down here for a change." Then as her aunt continued to look at her with a questioning frown, she said swiftly and almost defiantly, "I really came down to tell you I went downstairs and talked to Lisa this afternoon."

After a moment her aunt asked, "Why?" in a quiet voice.

"Because it was very important that I thank her for her present." As she answered, she remembered that she hadn't done that at all.

"In spite of the fact that I expressly asked you not to?"

Peggy nodded miserably. "I'm sorry I disobeyed you."

"You are always sorry—afterward," Aunt Emily commented drily. "Do I have any assurance that you will respect my wishes in the future? Will it be a waste of time to repeat that you are *not* under any circumstances to go down to visit her again?"

"I'll remember."

"There is absolutely no need for you to get involved with a girl like that—no, no arguments, Peggy." Her aunt held up a warning hand as Peggy began to protest. "I know you think her very nice, and I'm sure she is. But I repeat what I have told you before. You are not to be too friendly with her, and the only way to avoid that is not to see her. That is not asking too much of you, I'm sure."

"I'll remember," Peggy promised again and turned disconsolately toward the door. As she climbed the stairs she found herself thinking that Aunt Emily hadn't even appreciated that she had come voluntarily and admitted her disobedience.

Next time I won't tell her, she thought rebelliously and then remembered there wouldn't be a next time. She had promised.

"If only there was just *one* other person to talk to about things, someone who feels the same way I do," she said aloud as she reached her room and closed the door behind her. "It's so hard to be all alone." *If I were only home,* she thought again longingly.

But then she had to admit honestly that it hadn't been easy there either. And there she'd had Bill to help—and all her friends in church. But at least at home people loved her, while here nobody really cared about her.

Uncle Walter didn't seem to know she was in the house. Aunt Emily knew—but was only concerned that she keep a set of rules.

And Jane—she didn't know what Jane really thought about her. They didn't see one another during the school day. Even though sixth through eighth grades were in the same building, the levels were separate except for assemblies in the auditorium. The grades even had separate lunch hours. That meant she usually ate by herself with a book propped in front of her as a protective shield in case anyone thought she was lonely. She was, but she had made up her mind that nobody would know it.

It wasn't that she didn't want friends. But it was so hard to take the first step. Aunt Emily had seen to it that her clothes were like what everyone else wore. But she knew that she hadn't grown up wearing smart, sophisticated, *in* clothes, and that memory made her feel as though she were someone she wasn't—a Cinderella in fairy-godmother clothes.

And Jane thinks I'm not scared of anything!

The soft chime of the clock in the downstairs hall made her realize it was late and she still hadn't had her devotions. She looked at her Bible, feeling a curious reluctance even to pick it up. "It won't matter if I don't read just this once," she said to herself slowly. But the thought brought back memories of her first weeks here when she hadn't read her Bible for a long time and had suffered as a result.

In her heart she knew the real reason she hated to have devotions now was knowing that she was wrong not to have somehow in three months let *somebody* at school know she was a Christian. At first she had said she would wait until she got better acquainted. Then she had said she couldn't do anything that would make Aunt Emily angry if she heard about it. And she knew Jane would be furious if she said anything to her friends. But she had to admit that she had been afraid to say anything anyway and she had used Aunt Emily and Jane as an excuse.

Almost hating to turn to the Bible verse she had learned last summer, she did anyway. "For whoever is ashamed of Me and My words, of him the Son of man will be ashamed." She was the one the verse was talking about. Just as she was responsible for Uncle Walter because she lived in the same house with him, so she was responsible for letting the kids she went to school with know that being a Christian was the most important thing in the world.

"I guess it's a good thing I've still got six months left. It will take that long to make up for the three I've wasted already."

5

"If this were home, we'd be walking to school in coats and mittens and boots through real deep snow. I'm glad we're not." Peggy tipped her head to feel the warm sun on her face as they waited for Roger to bring around the car the first day back to school after Christmas vacation.

Jane shivered. "I'll never forget how cold it was when I was there. I thought I'd freeze to death before I got back home."

"Umm," Peggy replied absently, thinking it had been cold in many ways during Jane's brief visit and shivering a little now herself. It had been then she'd begun to be aware of the ugly undercurrents of trouble between her parents.

"I guess it's cold where Bill is," she went on thinking out loud.

"How does he get to school?"

"Bus, I think. Sometimes he walks when the weather is nice, but I'm sure he said there was a bus that picked up kids from the other farms."

"Does he really like living on a farm?" There was curiosity and disbelief in Jane's voice that made Peggy speak quickly and proudly in Bill's defense.

"That shows you don't know what Bill is like. He can get along anywhere with anyone any time."

"Well, sure, anyone could who didn't have any opinions of his own," Jane sniffed.

"Bill isn't like that!" Peggy answered hotly.

"I wouldn't know," Jane answered defensively. Then, as Peggy glared at her she said, "Well, after all, I've never known him as a brother. It's not my fault."

"I didn't say it was," Peggy answered coldly. She climbed into the car beside Jane, and they rode in silence to school.

"What time do you want to be picked up?" The chauffeur held the door for them as he asked.

"I've got a meeting after school for about an hour," Jane answered and looked at Peggy. "You don't have to wait for me."

Peggy shrugged. "I might as well. There's no use having the car come two different times."

"OK. About four then." With a brief "See you" to Peggy, Jane went off looking for Stella.

Peggy trudged up the broad walk to the steps of the building and climbed them slowly. All the courage she had felt that morning as she read her Bible and prayed for the willingness to live for the Lord that day seemed to be slipping away. In its place came a fear that made her hands moist and tightened her throat.

Maybe there won't be a chance to say anything, she said to herself almost hopefully, and that's the way it seemed all morning. The first class started immediately, and there was only time to run from one to the next before lunch.

When she reached the cafeteria, she stood in the long line and decided this was certainly the place and time if only she could find the right person. She thought her heart must be pounding loudly enough for everyone to hear. Swallowing hard, she turned and smiled at the girl behind her. "Are you glad to get back to school again?"

The girl stared back at her. "Are you kidding?" she asked coldly and turned away.

"Well, that's that." And with an odd feeling of relief,

40

Peggy selected what she wanted from the counter, found a table by herself, and concentrated on the book she had brought along as a defense against the loneliness of a solitary lunch.

As she ate and read, the conversation from the next table began to seep into her consciousness. "*Anyone* would be a welcome change from old Johnson. This one's real sharp looking. Know what I mean?"

"I'll say," was the answer. "Johnson always looked so crummy."

"Remember the time she wore that goofy outfit and Carol whistled at her?"

There was general laughter. "Yeah, she got the point all right. Turned red as a beet."

"How come she isn't coming back?"

"I heard she was sick. Anyway, it's a break for us."

"Yeah! If this one is any better."

"She is. I had gym first hour, and she was neat."

Peggy watched from under lowered lids as the girls finished their lunches, picked up their books, and sauntered off. So there was a new gym teacher. *I'll find out what she's like next hour. Not that a new teacher will make any difference as far as I'm concerned.*

She trailed the rest of the class onto the gym floor. The girls lined up along the south wall in response to the blast of the whistle. She knew the rest of the class was busy sizing up the new teacher too, and she liked what showed on the surface. Her figure was tall and slim. She had medium-long blonde hair with just a little curl at the ends, a face that wasn't terribly pretty but was very friendly. Her voice issued crisp orders in a tone that was very self-assured and, at the same time, very warm.

And Peggy, listening to Mrs. Tremont's brief introduction of herself, wondered wistfully if self-confidence like that came with years of experience or if one had to be born with it.

"—so I may be with you the rest of the year," Mrs. Tremont was finishing. She paused momentarily and looked around the circle of listening girls. "Miss Johnson has taken a leave of absence for health reasons due partly to some rather unpleasant experiences she had while teaching."

She waited until the undercurrent of murmuring had subsided, and then went on evenly, "I think it's only fair to tell you that I am not new at teaching. I taught here for three years before I was married. And I am not easily rattled." She waited again for complete attention. "When you hear this"—she blew a shrill blast on her whistle—"I want your instant attention." Then suddenly her face lighted with a smile that flashed a deep dimple in one cheek, and she finished, "I'm anticipating a good time, because I think gym is fun."

Peggy groaned as she followed the class into teams. Maybe gym was fun if you were good at it, but it certainly wasn't for her.

Just before the class ended Mrs. Tremont blew the whistle. "I'd like to see you a few at a time in my office so I can get acquainted with you individually as soon as possible. So will the following please stop in my office after school today unless you have some other activity scheduled?"

Peggy's name was included in the list. She noted mentally that all the others were not too sharp in gym activities either.

After her last class, she went down to the gym office, which was just beyond the lockers and dressing room. The class coming out crowded past in a rush, and Peggy saw Jane and Stella talking animatedly together.

"Hi. What are you doing down here?" Jane asked when she saw her.

"We're supposed to see the teacher." Peggy nodded after the others who had gone on into the office.

"What for? She read off some names in our class too."

"All the dumb ones," Stella added.

Peggy looked at her angrily. "She told us she was going to see *everybody.*"

"Oh, I guess she just started with the dumb ones—in our class, I mean," Stella said with a smirk that made Peggy want to slap her. "See you at four," she threw over her shoulder to Jane as she saw Mrs. Tremont close the office door.

She dashed across the locker room and opened the door timidly. "I'm supposed to be here, too," she said in answer to Mrs. Tremont's questioning look.

"Come in. I don't want to keep anyone very long, so I'll get to the point of this right away." She sat down and looked around with a smile as she picked up a sheet of paper from her desk. "Right now you are just a list of names to me, but I don't want you to stay that way all the rest of the year. I'll be asking different ones in each day until I have talked to everyone. I'm sure it's obvious to you why you were chosen first. I purposely picked the ones who, from the grades you've had, are not too keen on gym. Right?" Her friendly, questioning gaze went around the room, and Peggy nodded a half-embarrassed agreement along with the rest of the girls.

"I want you to learn to like it because it's good for you even though you may never excel in athletics. It's very easy for any of us to get an inferior feeling about something we don't do well. That in turn makes us nervous and unable to do as well as we really could. I know that's true of phys ed." She smiled around at them again. "Any questions?"

The girl standing next to her asked a question, but Peggy didn't hear it or the answer. Her attention had been caught by something on the desk, and she was straining to see if it really was what she thought it was. The back of the book was turned away from her and the cover was red instead of black, but it looked like it might be a Bible.

Her thoughts were interrupted by a movement among the girls at the other end of the room. One of them stepped over to the desk, said a few sentences, and then turned and went out. As the next one stepped up to the desk, Peggy looked at the girl beside her. "I wasn't listening," she whispered. "What are we supposed to do?"

"Go over individually, tell your name and what class you're in and one thing you especially like about gym— if anything."

Peggy looked around. She was next to the last in line. If she were last and nobody else was in the room—she looked at the girl again.

"Would you trade places with me?" she whispered.

"Sure, I'm in a hurry anyway."

The reference to time made Peggy look at her watch. Good. Only three-thirty. That would give plenty of time to finish here and not keep Jane waiting.

It was her turn, and she looked down into Mrs. Tremont's friendly face.

"You have to be either Martha Larson or Peggy Andrews since there are two names left on my list and only one girl. Which is it?"

"Peggy."

"And you're in the class right after lunch apparently. Is Martha busy or sick?"

"I don't know. I hardly know her."

"What do you like about gym?"

Peggy's mind whirled. She'd been so busy wondering

44

about Mrs. Tremont that she hadn't planned what to say. She hesitated and then blurted, "Really nothing."

Mrs. Tremont laughed. "Well, at least you're frank about it. Maybe I should have asked what you least disliked."

"Umm, I guess—I guess the exercises."

Mrs. Tremont made a notation beside Peggy's name as she said, "You're right in line with everyone else in this group, then. Maybe by June you'll be liking other things too. Thanks for stopping in, Peggy."

The note of finality in her voice made Peggy turn away with a last lingering glance at the desk. Should she ask about it? If she were wrong, Mrs. Tremont might be angry and have it in for her the rest of the year. But at least then she would have spoken to someone for that day. This was the very last opportunity to carry out her earnest prayer of the morning. She turned back with her hand poised over the doorknob.

"Mrs. Tremont?"

"Yes?"

"I—I was wondering—"

Mrs. Tremont waited a moment and then said encouragingly, "Yes?"

"Is that—do you have—what I mean is, I thought maybe that book on your desk was a Bible." She said the last words fearfully, not expecting Mrs. Tremont's face to light up so eagerly.

"Why, yes, it is!" She picked it up in both hands and held it for Peggy to see. "You have one too?"

"Yes. I read it every day. At least, I've read almost every day since I was saved."

"I'm a Christian too," Mrs. Tremont said simply with a smile.

Peggy let her breath out in a little sigh. She hadn't

expected to find a teacher who was a Christian! She smiled back, a trace of tears blurring her eyes.

"Tell me about yourself, Peggy. Where do you live, and when were you saved?"

"I'm living with my aunt and uncle just for this one year. Mr. and Mrs. Conway. They live out in Parkway. But I really live in Pennsylvania, and that's where I was saved almost a year ago. In fact it will be a year in a couple of months." She wondered if she should tell more but decided that was enough.

"This is wonderful, Peggy! I think God must have sent you here for a purpose."

Peggy looked at her blankly, and Mrs. Tremont leaned across her desk confidentially.

"I taught here for three years before I was married two years ago, and as far as I could discover there was absolutely not one other Christian in the whole school. Of course, I'm not allowed to talk to anyone about such things during school hours, but I did try during personal interviews like this but didn't get any response at all. And to think my first day back this time, you pop up."

"I'm really not a very good one." Peggy traced her finger along the edge of the desk as she made the admission.

"Are your relatives Christians?"

Peggy shook her head.

Mrs. Tremont nodded understandingly. "It's hard when you're all alone." She opened the Bible as she spoke and turned the pages. "I was wondering this morning as I got ready to come to school how I could live for God in a special way these next few months. I'm not allowed to talk about my faith in God, but that doesn't mean I can't *show* my faith by the way I live."

Peggy looked back, puzzled. "What do you mean?"

"Look here in Colossians two, verse six. God says we're

46

supposed to live for Him in the same way we were saved. See? 'As you received Christ Jesus the Lord, so walk in Him, ... established in the faith.'"

She looked up at Peggy, her eyes sparkling. "When I was saved I believed God has the power to forgive my sins. Now I believe He has the power to help me live for Him. He'll do that for you. And when you get discouraged, just remember that your faith is in *God,* not in yourself."

As Peggy looked down into her glowing face, someone knocked on the door. "Come in," Mrs. Tremont called. Peggy looked around as Jane walked in and said, "Peggy! We've been waiting and waiting!" her voice cross.

"I'm sorry. I forgot the time." She looked away from Jane whose gaze had gone from the open Bible to Mrs. Tremont and back to Peggy.

"This is my sister, Jane." It was too late to call back the word and say *cousin,* so she let it stand.

"Hello, Jane. I remember your face from class." It was merely a statement, but Peggy thought if Jane's face had looked as spoiled and petulant then as it did now, it was no wonder the teacher remembered her.

She turned to Mrs. Tremont and said, "Thank you."

"Thank you, Peggy. We must become very well acquainted in the next few months. Will you two be going home this summer?"

She looked from one to the other as she asked, and Jane answered stiffly, "I live here."

Peggy flushed with embarrassment and simply nodded her head.

"Did you have to tell her all the family secrets?" Jane demanded angrily as they hurried out to the car.

"I didn't tell her anything about the family. We only talked a few minutes."

"Everyone else has been gone a long time."

"I was the last one in line. Then I saw she had a Bible on her desk so I just talked a minute and told her I had one too."

"As though nobody else does!"

"So walk in Him, so walk in Him—" The words were a refrain that beat back the angry thoughts filling Peggy's mind.

"I'm not going to quarrel, Jane," she said, surprised at her even tone. "I'm sorry I kept you waiting. But I'm glad I talked to Mrs. Tremont, because I found that she's a Christian too."

She didn't know what reaction to expect but wasn't prepared for the expression that flitted across Jane's face. On anyone else it would have been envy.

6

The impossible has certainly happened, thought Peggy one afternoon a couple of months later as she dressed for gym. *To think that I of all people would really look forward to phys ed.*

It was all due to Mrs. Tremont, of course, and her contagious enthusiasm for her subject. Not that she worked the miracle of transforming everyone in her class into Olympic stars. Peggy still quaked when it was her turn to serve in volleyball and still needed every assist allowed in getting the ball over the net. But she was learning to take her failures a little more in stride and tried to improve.

More important was the lift in spirit she received from knowing someone else in school was a Christian. There wasn't much chance to talk to Mrs. Tremont except when Jane had a club meeting after school. But when they did visit, Peggy always had a list of questions.

She found it hard not to bubble over with quotations from Mrs. Tremont but tried to keep from doing so. Jane once said scornfully, "Don't you ever have any ideas of your own? It sounds like all you do is copy what *she* says."

"Well, what's wrong with that?" she snapped in answer, but Jane only walked away. The next time Peggy stopped in to see Mrs. Tremont she told her about her problems with Jane. "Sometimes I don't care whether she likes me or not."

"If people like *you*, they are more ready to listen to your opinions."

"Yes, but—" Peggy began.

Mrs. Tremont went on. "You should try to forget about yourself and whether or not you are making a good impression. The best way to get people to like you is to like them. Not only Jane, but others too."

"It's hard to forget about myself. I've always been self-conscious about my clothes and my looks and everything. And out here I'm even more self-conscious."

"You don't need to worry about your clothes." Mrs. Tremont eyed her primrose yellow jumper and frilly white blouse.

"Well, no, not these. But my aunt gave me all these clothes, and Jane knows it. She's probably told the other kids."

"Why would she? She wouldn't want anyone to know her sister didn't have nice clothes of her own."

Peggy looked at her in surprise. "Of course that's what she would think! How did you know how Jane is? That makes me feel better."

Mrs. Tremont continued to look at her thoughtfully. "Why are you so self-conscious about your looks?"

Peggy giggled. "I guess if you have to ask, maybe they're not so bad after all."

But she sobered when Mrs. Tremont didn't smile back. Instead she said,"I'm afraid we too often try to look and dress according to the standards of people whose values are different from ours. Do you want to be a movie actress?"

Peggy blinked in surprise at the abrupt question. "No—no, of course not," she stammered.

"Lots of Christian girls like you would be just as horrified at the question. And yet they spend too much time thinking of how they look and what to wear and the kind of impression their outside appearance will make on people."

"Yes, but—"

Mrs. Tremont smiled. "I know what you are going to say because I went through this problem too. And I felt the same way about it that you do. Well, maybe it wasn't as much of a problem for me, because I grew up in the country, and everyone in our small school and church had about the same amount of money and we all dressed pretty much alike. But when I went away to college it really hit me. I felt like the proverbial hayseed. I got mocked because my clothes weren't the *in* styles. And I cried buckets." She smiled as she spoke, but her eyes had a faraway expression that made Peggy wonder what memories she was seeing.

"But clothes and how you look *are* important!" Peggy was stubborn in her emphasis.

"Very."

"But you said—"

"No, I didn't. You just *expected* me to say they weren't important. They are, but not for the reason so many girls think." She paused and bit her lip reflectively.

"Maybe I could put it this way. Every Christian girl should want to be clean and well-dressed and attractive for her own self-image and for the testimony it will be to other people. Maybe this will explain what I mean. I pass a bakery every morning on the way to school. As much as I love pastries and cakes I would *never* buy any in that place. I suppose the things are delicious, but the windows are so dirty it's hard to see what's on display. And the paper on the shelves is spotted with crumbs. When I stop at that corner I usually look in—or try to. Maybe it doesn't bother some people, but for me the dirt spoils the product. I think that's an example of what we are talking about." She looked at Peggy, who nodded slowly.

"You mean we're like the window, and if we're not clean outside, what's inside can't be seen?"

Mrs. Tremont nodded. "But there's another side to it. Have you been downtown much?"

"Some."

"Do you know that store right across the street from the telephone company?"

"You mean the one that has such beautiful decorations in the windows?"

"Yes. What do they sell?"

"Well, I—I don't know," Peggy floundered. "I never notice especially because I always look at the decorations."

"Exactly." Mrs. Tremont smiled up at her.

Peggy frowned. "I don't think I know what you're getting at."

"I'm sure the owners want to sell their products, and the decorations are only supposed to make people come in and buy. But lots of people don't. They stop and admire the outside, but they never go inside to buy the product. They scarcely know what is being sold."

"I guess so," Peggy agreed slowly.

"But you don't see how that applies to you?"

"Well, no."

"Who do you think is the best-dressed and prettiest girl in school?"

"Janet Ferguson," Peggy replied promptly. "If I could only look like her!" she added fervently.

"She does have curly hair and a pretty face."

"And it's natural, too. Her hair, I mean. And her eyelashes are so long and thick." Peggy's voice was frankly envious as she looked from Mrs. Tremont to stare with regret at her own reflection in the mirror behind the desk.

"What's she like?" Mrs. Tremont's voice was casual enough, but Peggy looked at her sharply.

"I don't know. We're only in history together, and she sits on the other side of the room. And, of course, she never talks to me," Peggy finished matter-of-factly.

"Why not?"

"Well, because I'm not in her group."

"Oh?"

"I mean, after all!"

"Why don't you try to be friends with her?"

"Me? With Janet Ferguson?" Peggy laughed. "Why would she want to be friends with me?"

"Maybe if you got acquainted you would like each other. Why don't you try this week to find out what she's like? You know, sort of hang around where she is and listen in on conversations, things like that."

"Someone as pretty and rich as she is wouldn't want to bother with me. She has a ton of friends already."

"Does she? Well, maybe you'll be friends too. You'll never know unless you try."

Mrs. Tremont's voice was so insistent that Peggy finally said, "I'll try, but I know it won't work."

Peggy did try for a few days, but that was all she could stand. "She's not a bit nice!" she reported back indignantly. "She cheats all the time in tests and then tries to lie out of it by pretending to blink tears away with those long eyelashes. And she's not popular after all."

Mrs. Tremont smiled understandingly at Peggy's disillusionment. "You see, you were dazzled by the decorations and didn't look to see what the product was."

"Yes, but I still wish I looked different."

"I suppose all girls wish their hair was different than it is. But after all, any nitwit can learn to roll hair or get a good cut. And even straight hair is pretty if it's clean and well-brushed."

"I know! Aunt Emily read me the riot act—" Peggy stopped, her face flaming with embarrassment. Here she was telling the family secrets after all. But when Mrs. Tremont didn't ask any questions she went on, "Aunt Emily is a very fastidious person and can't stand anyone with dirty fingernails or a wrinkled dress."

"Three cheers for your aunt," Mrs. Tremont commented drily.

"Yes, but then she doesn't care at all about things that are really important, like being saved," Peggy protested indignantly.

"Would she be more apt to listen to a person with dirty fingernails talk about being a Christian than to one who was clean?"

"Well, no. But then I don't think that she would listen at all to anyone." Then Peggy looked away, embarrassed as she mumbled, "Of course, I haven't said anything to her directly about what I believe. But I'm sure she knows—I think."

Mrs. Tremont looked at her seriously. "Peggy, I wish I had known when I was your age that there are two kinds of beauty. One is outside, the other is inside. And we should try to have both. Do try to be as attractive as you possibly can. This means shining clean hair—a super figure by dieting and exercising—only enough makeup to add a sheen. Your appearance won't be what brings your aunt to know the Lord, but it may make her willing to listen in the first place."

She stopped, her slender fingers gesturing expressively. "But remember that outer beauty doesn't last. We get old—gray—wrinkled. Age does have a beauty of its own, but only if we have learned to develop the inner beauty. The Bible calls it having 'a meek and gentle spirit' and knowing 'the joy of the Lord' and experiencing 'the peace that passes all understanding.' This is the kind of beauty that will shine out and light up you and everyone around you."

"I'll try," Peggy said soberly, terribly impressed by the seriousness of Mrs. Tremont's voice.

When she got home from school, she found a letter from Bill, the first he had written in a month. He began abruptly without a greeting.

It's happened. Peggy, I can hardly believe it's true, but Uncle Ed is saved! It happened this morning while we were doing chores. I've been getting up extra early to help him in the mornings because he hasn't been feeling well lately. We'd just finished milking when he said he wanted to tell me something. He said he didn't hold much with this business of going to church, had always thought it was a waste of time, but lately he'd been thinking it over and decided he'd like to go regularly, too. He said the trouble was he didn't know much about God. Then he began to cry. Imagine! Uncle Ed! It kind of scared me. And then he put his head down and said, "God, if You know all about me and still want me, then here I am." That was his prayer. And that's it.

When we went in for breakfast, he told Aunt Mary about it. She looked surprised at first, but then she laughed and said it was bound to happen with me around talking religion. She said she didn't agree with him or me, but she'd never yet told him what he should or shouldn't do and she wasn't going to start now. So maybe it won't be long until she is saved too. It's sure wonderful how God works things out, isn't it, Peg?

Hope everything is going OK out your way. I'm beat. This is about the longest letter I've ever written. This pen you sent for Christmas is neat. Thanks again.

Bill

Peggy held the letter in both hands and frowned down at it. It *was* wonderful, and no more than she expected. Bill couldn't have lived very long with Uncle Ed without his being saved. Of course, Uncle Ed was different from Uncle Walter. He was—she searched for the right word—simpler. That was it. When you were rich like Uncle Walter it was harder to believe. And yet—she remembered Bill had written before about Uncle Ed. He had been pretty well satisfied with his life too, so maybe it wasn't any easier after all for him to say yes to God.

"One thing I know for sure," she said aloud. "If Bill had lived in this house as long as I have, Aunt Emily and Uncle Walter would have known for certain what he believes." Remembering the last part of the conversation with Mrs. Tremont, she added, "He would have let them know in such a nice way they would like him better because of his beliefs."

There wasn't anything at all about Bill that got in the way of letting other people know about the Lord Jesus. That's just what Mrs. Tremont meant. Bill would have hooted at the idea of his having "inner beauty," but he had it just the same. That's what Uncle Ed had seen.

Peggy knelt beside her bed. She had already prayed that morning for her parents and aunt and uncle and Jane. She knew at the time that they had been form words said from habit. But this time she really *prayed* for the people God had sent her to live with for this one year out of her life.

The wind blowing in through the open window ruffled the pages of her Bible to a leaf in the back where she had copied a few lines from a poem Mrs. Tremont had once quoted. She didn't know the name of the poem or who had written it, but she couldn't forget the lines.

Help me to walk so close to Thee,
That those who know me best can see

> I live as godly as I pray,
> And Christ is real from day to day.

She read the words silently. They were so easy to say but so hard to live. Yet she knew she wanted them to be true of her.

7

She woke the next morning, remembering the poem. Today she would put it to work. She dressed and ran downstairs, almost colliding with Jane as she pushed into the breakfast room.

"Hi. What are you doing today?"

"Stella and I were going swimming today at the club, but now she can't. A whole Saturday wasted!" Jane scowled with disappointment.

"Can't *we* go?" Peggy invited herself swiftly.

"Umm—well—" Jane looked at her doubtfully, and Peggy knew she was thinking what an embarrassment she would be in front of other people. Then she seemed to make an abrupt decision. "OK, if you want to. I'll tell Miss Murphy she'll have to take us after all."

"I'll just grab some breakfast," Peggy yelled after Jane. She gulped a glass of orange juice and reached for a bowl of cereal.

Jane came back and flopped into a chair. "Don't rush. Miss Murphy can't take us. She's got some work to do. But she said Father is going golfing at the club and we can go with him and eat lunch there."

"What time?"

"About an hour."

"What do you wear at a country club?"

Jane shrugged. "Nothing special. Just wear shorts and

a shirt. That lavender outfit looks good on you. Meet you later."

Peggy nodded, munching the cereal, mentally phrasing a letter to Alice in which she would say casually, "Oh, by the way, we went swimming at a ritzy club today."

She thought of the letters she had written Alice since last June—ten at least. And she'd only received one in return. And that had been just a skinny one page with no news about anyone. She frowned out across the sloping lawn. "I wonder if Ann ever sees her around school? I'll ask her the next time I write."

She took the back stairs two at a time, something she didn't dare do up the Cinderella staircase, and got her suit. She was kind of scared of the kids she might meet at the pool, but at least she had a swimsuit that she looked good in. It had just enough padding in the top to make it look as though she were more than just a straight-up-and-down stick.

Uncle Walter gave Roger directions to drop them off at the entrance to the dressing rooms. "Have a good time. Meet me in the lounge in two hours."

Peggy was glad she could just tag along after Jane who knew the ropes. She was glad too that there were very few people in the pool yet and no one their age. She still felt like a poor kid masquerading as a rich kid in spite of Mrs. Tremont's lectures.

Peggy paddled around in the shallow end, practicing the little she knew about swimming and envying Jane's self-assurance.

"I wish I could swim the way you do."

"You could if you tried," Jane said with impatience in her voice.

Peggy turned to face her, hanging on to the edge of the pool. "Do you remember telling me you didn't think I was scared of anything?"

"Yeah."

"Well, I am, and this is one of them. I'm scared of water. I really get panicky. And you're one of the first persons I've ever admitted that to. That's why I haven't practiced in the pool at the house."

Jane ducked under the water and came up, wiping her face. She looked around. "Why don't you practice now when there's hardly anyone around?"

"People are probably watching from inside—"

"So what? They don't know who you are—or care." She pushed off as she said, "Just do this." She turned and swam off a few yards, then turned and came back.

As Peggy hesitated, afraid she couldn't do it, Jane said impatiently, "If you're always afraid to try anything because you're scared you can't do it, then you never will."

Peggy bit back the sharp defensive words that sprang to her lips. Instead she said, "OK—show me again."

Jane swam off a short distance again and came back. "I'll do it once more and stay out there while you come out to me."

Peggy watched carefully and then tried to kick her legs the way Jane did. To her surprise she found she was able to make it out to where Jane treaded water, waiting for her.

"You see," Jane said triumphantly, "all you have to do is try."

Peggy kicked her way back and held onto the side of the pool. This could be fun once she got the hang of it. "I'm going to stay in the shallower end for a little while and practice," she said and added, "Thanks, Jane."

Jane watched her go back and forth a few times and then swam away. Peggy was enjoying herself so much she didn't notice that the pool was filling up. She came up from ducking, feeling quite satisfied with her efforts, and looked into Stella's face.

"Hi!"

"Hello," Stella answered.

Jane looked at Peggy's surprised expression and explained, "After we left she called because she found she could go swimming after all, and she came with her dad. He's playing golf too."

Suddenly Peggy found herself floundering in the water and thrashed wildly around, grabbing out to hang on to the side of the pool. "I—I guess I'd better go back where it isn't so deep," she finally gasped.

"Oh, Peggy!" Jane exclaimed. "Don't give up now." Then to Stella she said, "I've been helping her learn to swim."

"She needs help?"

Peggy felt herself flush. The last time she had been swimming with Jane and Stella she had taken Stella's dare to go down the high slide, which was restricted to good swimmers only. She had to force back angry words and made herself say, "Oh, well, I'm learning," hard as it was to sound cool.

They looked around at the bunch of little kids dashing toward the shallow end of the pool, their voices shrill with excitement.

"They're going to take over," Stella complained. "Come on, I'll race you across and back once, Jane. Why don't you come too, Peggy?"

There was no mistaking the sneering challenge in her voice. Before Peggy could think of an answer that would be a good put-down for Stella, Jane said, "OK. The first one back has to touch Peggy."

As they took off, Peggy hoisted herself up to the edge of the pool. She watched them race to the other side and turn back. Stella was a little ahead all the way, and Peggy yelled encouragement to Jane, who spurted enough to touch Peggy's outstretched hand first.

Stella climbed out, shaking the water from her short hair. "It's time to get dressed for lunch anyway. Dad told me to meet him at one sharp."

Peggy followed them and showered and dressed, hoping Stella wouldn't ask if she could eat with them. But when they got to the lounge, she saw Uncle Walter waiting for them and two other men with him.

"We're ready." Jane tucked her arm in his as she spoke.

"Good. We've got a table waiting." Uncle Walter motioned to the dining room hostess, who smiled and came toward them.

"We're all having lunch together." Peggy knew it was Stella's father who spoke because of the strong resemblance between them.

They were seated in the dining room at a round table, the three girls together, with Uncle Walter and the other two men across from them. Peggy couldn't bring herself to bow her head in front of everyone even though she wanted to. As a substitute she unfolded her napkin slowly and spread it out in her lap as she said a brief, "Thank You, God."

After they had ordered, the men continued the conversation they had started earlier. "I don't expect you to be convinced," she heard Stella's father say. "Personally, I'm beginning to think there may be something to this Christianity business after all. The kind this fellow is preaching, anyway. It's different from what I usually doze through in *our* church, Walter."

Peggy had reached for her water glass but stopped. Stella's parents went to the same church her aunt and uncle did. She saw Uncle Walter shake his head. "I get enough religion Sunday morning. That's the way I like it, and that's all I need."

But Mr. Hamilton went on. "I know. That's what I've

always thought too. But when I heard this fellow—well, he's *almost* got me convinced."

Uncle Walter snorted in disgust. "How can a sensible, level-headed man like you be taken in by a lot of nonsense?"

The third man spoke for the first time. "It's not a lot of nonsense, Walter. It's the real thing."

Stella's dad looked at him. "You really believe all this business about a personal God, about people needing to be—saved?" He dropped his voice as he said the word, glancing around in evident embarrassment.

The other man's voice was positive. "Absolutely."

"Since when?"

"A couple of weeks ago." He hesitated a moment and then gave a short laugh. "Frankly, this is the first time I've admitted it to anyone. Haven't even told Lucy yet. She'll probably laugh."

"She should," Uncle Walter grunted. "It won't last. It can't. It's not practical."

"Why not?" the other man challenged.

"You can't believe in that kind of Christianity and be a good businessman. I'm not down on the church. It does a lot of good in the world. I *am* against this radical nonsense that says, 'Love your enemies.' You can't get ahead in the world that way."

"I'm going to find out," the other man answered.

Peggy had listened to the conversation, feeling her heart pound with excitement. She had never dreamed God might use this way to make Uncle Walter listen. She liked this man, whoever he was, and Stella's father too.

Uncle Walter changed the conversation—purposely, Peggy thought—and the men spent the rest of the meal discussing politics. When they finished lunch, Stella, her father, and the other man went off, the two men talking together earnestly while Uncle Walter signed the bill for the lunch.

As they went to the driveway where Roger waited with the car, Peggy asked, "Who was that other man?"

"You know Janet Ferguson? It's her dad."

Peggy felt shock. Janet Ferguson's father! God certainly was able to work miracles. There was hope for Uncle Walter after all if he would only listen to his friends. If she prayed for him and his friends talked to him, he could be saved in spite of himself.

She looked at Janet the next Monday with new interest in spite of her feeling of dislike and lingered after history until Janet came out of the room. "Hi," she said nervously.

"Well, hi," was the disinterested reply.

"I—I met your father Saturday."

"How exciting." Janet's bored voice brought a flush to Peggy's face.

"He's nice," she finished lamely.

Janet shrugged. "He's OK." She walked off with a not-so-low comment to the girls with her. "What's with her?"

Peggy looked after her resentfully. A lot of good it did to try to be friendly with someone like that!

8

In spite of Peggy's hopes, the weeks went by without any change in anyone. The routine of each day went on as usual. Then Peggy became aware of the excitement in school as plans for the annual spring festival got into full swing. Posters appeared in home rooms, and notices went up on the hall bulletin boards advertising it.

Peggy couldn't work up much enthusiasm because she didn't know what the festival was like, and she didn't know anything about the plans. She got put on the costume committee, but only as a substitute, and she hadn't been to any meetings. The last week in April the faculty adviser of that committee called her in to explain that one of the members was sick and she would have to fill her place.

She was glad it was a committee she knew something about, even though she wasn't crazy about some of the others who were on it. She was less enthusiastic than ever after sitting in on her first committee meeting. The whole time was spent arguing over the costume for the lead part. The one whose place Peggy had taken had pushed through an idea she and Janet had had. Now that she wasn't there, some of the other girls wanted the idea changed completely.

"There isn't time," Janet argued. "And anyway, I'm supposed to have that part, and I don't want it messed up at the last minute."

"It won't mess things up," Sally insisted. "I've been telling you all along that costume will look creepy."

"Not on Janet! Nothing, but *nothing* could look creepy on her!"

Janet looked coldly at the mocking voice. "Maybe you think you can do this part better than I can!" she snapped.

The other girl shrugged. "I don't think it. I know it."

"Well, you're not going to get the chance!"

Peggy had been looking at the design for the costume and privately thought it would look creepy on anyone.

"What's it supposed to be?" she ventured timidly.

"There! You see?" Sally was triumphant. "Nobody will be able to tell what you're supposed to represent."

"Anyone with any sense can tell!" Janet snapped again. She snatched up the design as the bell rang for class and stormed out.

"Honestly, she makes me sick!" Sally's voice showed her disgust.

"She always thinks she knows so much," someone else chimed in.

"Just because she's got the lead she thinks she can boss everything!"

"What *is* she supposed to be?" Peggy asked again.

Sally looked at her. "Can't you really tell? I thought you were trying to needle her."

"No, I don't know what the thing is all about. Is it a play? Or a musical?"

The final bell rang, and Sally jumped up quickly. "We'd better run. Here's a copy of the script. Give it back before our meeting tomorrow. And listen, kids. Back me up on this, or Janet will have it all her way. See you tomorrow."

Peggy read through the play before dinner and thought it was awfully clever. But she mentally brought

68

up a picture of the costume for the lead part. It wasn't right, and she frowned over it, wondering why. She reached for a pencil and paper from the night table, propped a magazine against her knee, and drew a few tentative lines.

The chimes interrupted her, but as soon as dinner was over she hurried back to her room, her mind trying to hold onto the vague idea flitting around in it. Frowning at what she had already tried, she tossed the papers into the wastebasket and tried again. Each attempt landed with the first until all of a sudden the idea began to take shape and the graceful lines of a dress swirled on paper.

A knock on the door and Jane's voice calling, "Peggy?" made her thrust the sketches under the pillow and toss the pencil at the night stand. It missed and fell on the floor, rolling under the bed as Jane pushed the door open.

"What're you doing?"

"Sitting. Nothing. Thinking."

"Same thing," Jane replied smartly in the friendlier tone she'd been using lately. Then her sharp eyes spotted the corner of the paper, which had not been pushed far enough under the pillow.

"What's this?" She pounced as she asked and pulled at the papers.

"Nothing. Don't!" Peggy grabbed for them, not wanting to be laughed at.

"How neat! Where'd you get these sketches?"

Peggy looked at her, not sure she had heard right.

"I like this one. Are they doll clothes?"

Peggy shook her head wordlessly.

"Who did them?" Jane demanded again and Peggy managed a weak, "I did."

"You're fooling!" Jane's look was skeptical. "Do another one."

Peggy searched on the floor for the pencil, tore a sheet of paper off the pad, and moved over to sit at the desk. Jane watched over her shoulder as she drew a design for a dress with a full swirling skirt.

"Hey, that's neat! I didn't know you could do stuff like this." Jane's voice was frankly admiring and made Peggy's head swim.

"How come you haven't drawn stuff like this before?"

"I didn't know I could. I've always drawn clothes for paper dolls when I was a kid, but that's different."

"What made you do these?"

"Oh, I was just fooling around." Then as Jane continued to look at the designs, she added carelessly, "I'm on the costume committee for the festival—"

"I didn't know that," Jane broke in.

"Well, originally I was just a substitute. But someone got sick so I'm a regular member."

"And you're supposed to design the costumes?"

"No!" Peggy reached for the sketches as she spoke, tore them in two, and tossed them in the wastebasket.

"What's the matter? What did you do that for?"

"Because!" Peggy answered shortly. Then, glancing at Jane's face, she was ashamed of her burst of anger. "It's just that the costumes are all designed, but some of the kids on the committee don't think one of them is right. Janet Ferguson likes it, and what she says goes, I guess."

"Are the costumes all made up?"

"Some of them are. But not Janet's. And hers is the one that isn't right."

Jane got up. "Oh, well! She usually gets her own way. 'Night."

Peggy tossed for a long time that night before she finally got to sleep. The sketches danced before her almost mockingly. But she knew she would never have enough nerve to show them to the rest of the committee, no matter how much Jane praised them. Janet already had the costume idea sewed up.

The committee met the next day during lunch hour, this time with the adviser. Sally burst into the meeting late with a gasped, "Sorry, someone stopped me."

"Janet's costume must go to the seamstress by tomorrow at the very latest," Miss Brown said emphatically. "She is almost through with the others and will just have time to do this last one without having to rush."

"Are you satisfied with the costume?" Sally asked politely.

Miss Brown shrugged. "It will do. I know some of you don't like it, but since no one has come up with a better idea, we had better go with it."

"I have a better idea," Sally said with a triumphant glance at Janet.

"What is it?"

"This." Sally opened her notebook and pulled out four sheets of paper that had been torn in two and then mended with tape.

Peggy reached for them with a muffled, "Oh, no!"

Sally coolly held them out of her reach and went on, "Don't you think one of these might do, Miss Brown?"

The adviser looked them over and nodded appreciatively. She held one out. "This one especially is better than any idea we have seen so far. Where did you get them?"

"From Peggy's cousin. That's why I was late to the meeting. She was waiting for me and said Peggy drew them last night and then threw them away. She got them out of the wastebasket this morning. I think they're *real* good."

"Show us how you do it, Peggy," someone suggested, and Miss Brown agreed. "This one is the best, but the tear comes across the skirt and it's difficult to see just how it should look."

Peggy tore a sheet of paper from her notebook and sketched another dress, her fingers trembling.

"Very nice." Miss Brown eyed it critically. "Better than the first. What do the rest of you think?" She looked around at the committee

There was general agreement from almost everyone.

"What about you, Janet? You have to wear it."

"Well, if everyone else thinks her idea is so good, I suppose we'll have to do it," she answered in a sulky voice.

"That's that, then," Miss Brown said briskly. "Now we can get to work. Peggy, the first thing will be for you to go to the art room after your last class and get a large sheet of poster paper. Do your design on it large enough that the seamstress can see it clearly. When you have finished bring it to me—no, I have to leave right after school. If you finish it this afternoon, leave it in the art room in a drawer and then bring it to me tomorrow before your first class."

Everything had happened so quickly, Peggy hadn't had time to wonder why Jane had rescued the sketches and brought them to Sally. Now as the meeting ended and she raced down to the lunchroom for a quick bite, a warm feeling of affection for Jane welled up inside her. As she reached the cafeteria door, Jane was waiting before going to her next class.

"Oh, hi," she said carelessly, "are you just now coming for lunch?"

"Thanks, Jane," Peggy answered softly.

"For what?"

"You know. For bringing the sketches and giving them to Sally."

"Oh, that!" Jane shrugged indifferently. Then, showing she really did care, she asked, "What happened?"

"Everybody thought they were good," Peggy answered, still not quite believing it herself. "Well, almost everybody. Janet didn't, of course. It was Miss Brown who really saved the day."

"I told you they were good. That's why I went into your room this morning after you had gone down to breakfast and got them."

"How did you know who to give them to?"

"I met Janet and asked who was in charge of the costume committee." She giggled suddenly. "If she'd known why I was asking, she never would have told me."

"I have to go up to the art room and do an enlargement so I won't be ready to go right after school."

"OK. I'll tell Roger to come back for you."

Peggy gulped down a malt and hamburger and raced for her next class. The world was a *wonderful* place! And Jane was pretty nice too.

She had been working only a few minutes in the art room after school when Jane came in. "I'll wait too. I told Roger to come back for us at four."

Peggy tried to hide her surprise. A few months ago Jane wouldn't have bothered to wait. She worked swiftly but carefully, wanting the design to be just right. Jane leaned over the drawing board with her chin cupped in her hand and watched as the lines swirled gracefully under Peggy's fingers. After she had watched for a while she began to wander around the room commenting on some of the artwork exhibited on the walls.

"What's in here?" she asked, her hand on a door knob.

Peggy looked around. "Sort of a storeroom and the place we wash our brushes and things."

Jane pulled the door open, peeked in, and then went inside.

In a few minutes Peggy looked around as the art room door opened again. Her heart beat faster as Janet and the girl who had supported her in the meeting came in. Janet walked determinedly over to Peggy and stood looking at her, her hands on her hips. She was obviously seething with anger.

"I hope you don't think you're going to get away with this!" she blazed.

"What?" Peggy asked nervously.

"This!" Janet stormed. "You and your ideas! I'm going to see to it that your dumb idea doesn't get submitted tomorrow."

Peggy looked helplessly toward the clean-up room, and Janet sneered, "Oh, don't waste your time trying to pretend that Mrs. Miller is in there. I know she's not. We waited around until we saw her get in her car and drive off." She snatched up a bottle of red ink as she spoke and went on furiously. "I'm going to splash this all over your fancy design and then keep you from doing another."

"I don't think you'd better." Jane's cool voice came from the doorway of the storage room. Jane stared at Janet with that cold, superior expression Peggy had hated so much when she first saw it, but which looked wonderful to her now.

Janet slowly put down the bottle of ink, turned, tight-lipped, and followed her friend to the door. She looked back at them as Jane left her position in the doorway and went over to stand with Peggy.

"OK, you win!" The door slammed behind them.

"Honestly, Jane, if you hadn't been here she would have ruined the whole thing!" Peggy exclaimed gratefully.

"Well, sure, if you'd let her. You have to learn to stand

up for yourself, Peggy," Jane said almost crossly. "Just because you're a Christian doesn't mean you have to let everybody walk all over you."

"That doesn't have anything to do with it," Peggy objected. Then at the stubborn expression on Jane's face, she tried to explain again how uncertain she felt about herself. But Jane only shook her head.

"Nobody likes to be around someone who's afraid to stick up for what she believes," she said in her stubborn voice.

Peggy finished her sketch in silence, thinking about what Jane had just said.

I'm going to try it, she resolved. *And on her, too!* And a tiny smile turned up the corners of her lips.

9

Jane spilled out the story of Peggy's sketches to Aunt Emily and Uncle Walter that evening at the dinner table.

"You really should see what she can do," she finished eagerly.

"Well, Peggy. I didn't know you had such talent."

Peggy felt herself flushing with pleasure at the warmth in her aunt's voice.

"It really isn't so much," she said, trying to be modest but at the same time being glad she excelled in something her aunt approved of.

"Janet Ferguson is sure steamed up at Peggy," Jane went on.

"Steamed up?" Aunt Emily frowned, and Jane bit her lip. "*Where* did you pick up such an expression?"

"Oh, everyone says things like that!"

"What does it mean?"

"Well, mad—"

"Mad?"

"Angry then," Jane said a little impatiently.

"Why was she angry?" Aunt Emily went on questioning.

"Because Peggy had a better idea than she did."

"There must have been more to it than that," Aunt Emily observed. "We know the Fergusons well."

Jane shook her head obstinately, and Peggy decided she should do some of the explaining too.

"It's just that I'm new on the costume committee, and Miss Brown took my idea for the lead part when Janet thought hers had already been decided on. That's all there was to it. Of course, I guess I'd have been mad—I mean, angry—if I'd been in her place," she added generously.

"The Fergusons are coming for dinner tomorrow evening," her aunt said. "I hope everything will be smoothed over by then."

Peggy and Jane looked at each other, but neither said anything.

Later that evening Jane came into Peggy's room in her pajamas and flopped on the empty twin bed.

"Are you writing another letter?"

"Umhm—to Bill."

After a moment Jane said in an offhand way, "Say hello to him for me."

Peggy looked up, startled, and half-turned in her desk chair to stare at Jane picking polish off her thumbnails. Then trying to be nonchalant too, she said, "OK." She'd been telling Bill what had happened at school and the excitement of her success had filled the letter with exclamation points. Now she sobered and continued.

You'll never believe what has just happened. Jane just came in (which she never used to do) without even asking if she could (which is also surprising because we used to keep our doors closed, which shows you just how perfectly *awful* things were around here at first) and— what was I talking about?—oh, yes, when she found out I was writing you she asked me to say hello for her. Imagine! She's never acted as though she cared at all about you before. She's the funniest person. One minute I simply can't stand her and then other times I feel sorry for her. And tonight I like her. She really helped me out today. I know that's a selfish reason for liking someone, but when she's

78

been so awful and then does something nice, it's easier to like her. And I really *want* to like her.

She finished the letter quickly and pulled open the drawer of the bedside table. "I'm sending Bill a couple of these pictures you took of me in the pool. He'll never believe that I'm in the water up to my neck and not yelling, 'Help!'"

She stuck the pictures in the envelope and licked it shut. She looked across at Jane. "Want to go down and play a game of Ping-Pong?"

"OK. But I want to ask you something first." Jane had that challenging stare that Peggy dreaded. "How come you keep your Bible in the drawer?"

"Well—I don't know." She made circles on the edge of a piece of stationery.

"You're nervous." Jane made the flat statement and added, "You always doodle like that when you don't know what to answer."

"How do you know?"

"I've watched you. It's a dead giveaway." Then, before Peggy could flounder out an answer, she jumped up. "Let's go play. You can drop your letter on the way."

Peggy followed Jane down to the front hall and propped the letter against the vase of roses. As she looked around at Jane she saw her standing with her finger against her lips. Uncle Walter's voice came from the living room, unusually loud. "I tell you, he won't drink it."

"Nonsense!" Aunt Emily's voice was positive. "I've never known Jim Ferguson to turn down a cocktail."

"He does now. I had lunch with him this noon. He wouldn't touch anything but coffee. He doesn't even smoke his pipe anymore."

"Why not?"

Uncle Walter cleared his throat. "He doesn't say exactly. Something about he'd been converted or some such nonsense. He's been quoting a preacher he has listened to recently."

"Oh." Aunt Emily dismissed the subject in a scornful voice. "Lucy will see to it that he doesn't hold any such silly notions as that very long. She'll keep him in check. With her at his elbow he'll drink his usual quota."

Peggy looked at Jane, wondering what she thought about Aunt Emily's words. How awful of her to want to encourage Mr. Ferguson to drink. But Jane only motioned her to follow and ran down to the family room. Peggy always felt like laughing at that description—"family room." It meant people doing things together, and that wasn't true of this house.

She picked up her paddle, knowing this was one thing she was good at from all the games they had played at church parties. Soon she had won two games and waited for Jane to serve for the third. Instead Jane held her paddle and asked abruptly, "Why would Mr. Ferguson stop drinking? You heard what they said about his listening to a preacher. Does that mean it's wrong to drink? I mean, of course it's different if a person gets *drunk*. But my folks don't. They just drink wine and champagne like everyone else does. What's wrong with that?"

Peggy turned the ball around and around in her fingers until Jane said, "You're doing that instead of doodling, and it means you don't have an answer."

"OK. All I can say is that there are certain things you don't do if you let God control your life. That's what my minister says. And drinking is one of them."

"How can you tell what's right and wrong to do? Isn't getting mad at other people wrong? Isn't being selfish wrong? And talking about other people?"

"Sure."

"How can you stop doing those things?"

80

"Just like Mr. Ferguson is doing. Letting God change you."

Jane looked across the table at her for a moment and then gave a slashing serve. Peggy missed the return and most of the others, and Jane won the game. They stopped to get a cold drink before going upstairs. All Jane said was, "See you," before she went into her room.

Peggy went into her room and shut the door, leaning against it, her face sober. Then she walked over, pulled open the drawer, and put her Bible out on top of the table.

The next evening at dinner when the maid reached to fill his wine glass, Mr. Ferguson looked up with a smile and a quiet, "No, thanks."

The annoyed look on his wife's face was apparent to everyone, but she said nothing. Later when he refused a second time, she said, "You'll have all our friends thinking you are sick."

"I've never felt better." He smiled at her and then turned to Uncle Walter and changed the subject.

Now, I would have gotten mad and either frozen up or said something that would have made other people mad too, Peggy thought. *I've got to learn how to stand up for what I believe in a nice way like that.*

When dinner was over Mrs. Ferguson said to Janet, "If you girls want to talk, go ahead. We won't be staying late. Your father is not very good company. Emily, I would like another glass of wine."

Janet followed Jane up the stairs with Peggy trailing behind. "Come on in. I'll put on a record," Jane threw over her shoulder as she went ahead of them into her room.

"My dad's been on my case about my records all of a sudden." Janet's voice showed her disgust. "I don't know why, when he's the one who bought some of them for me. He wants me to listen to 'uplifting' stuff." She rolled her eyes and made a face.

What a dumb evening, Peggy thought. Jane had put on a record, not loud but too loud for them to talk. Anyway, there wasn't anything to talk about. Janet was in eighth grade so she didn't know many of Jane's friends. And she totally ignored Peggy.

Just before Janet left, Jane said bluntly, "Janet, I'm the one who brought those sketches to school and gave them to Sally. Peggy didn't know anything about it. She wasn't even going to bring them. So don't be mad at her."

Peggy stared open-mouthed, listening as Jane went on. "After all, Peggy can't help it if she's talented like that, and it certainly wasn't her fault Miss Brown liked them."

Janet shrugged. "I hope you don't think I've lost any sleep over a little thing like that. After all, I have the lead part, and that's a whole lot more important than who designs the costumes. Nobody's going to care who did that."

"Of course not," Jane agreed and winked at Peggy behind Janet's back.

After she had gone and Peggy was ready for bed, she crossed the hall to Jane's room and knocked.

"Come in," Jane called.

"I just wanted to thank you," Peggy said.

Jane was already in bed. "That's OK. I thought it should be said." She hesitated a moment and then, without looking at Peggy, she slid down, pulled up the sheet and turned off the light almost in one motion. "After all, sisters should stick together," came her low voice from the darkness. "Good-night."

Peggy backed out and closed the door gently. She found tears sliding down her cheeks even while she knew she was smiling foolishly. Jane had said they were sisters!

10

The rest of the month flew by, and Peggy knew she was happier than she had been at any time since coming west. The spring festival was scheduled for the end of May. Although Peggy was not needed at any of the rehearsals, her opinions were important since her design was being used, in spite of what Janet thought. Where formerly people in the lunchroom had simply ignored her, now the few girls on the spring festival committee smiled at her with genuine interest. Sally included her in her crowd and made room for her at their table every day.

Life at home was much nicer too, now that Jane had thawed. But Peggy still found herself getting ruffled when Jane sounded off as though *she* were the older sister.

"You know, Peggy," she said one evening a week before the festival was to be given, "if you ask me, you're getting too chummy with Sally and her bunch."

"Well, I didn't ask you," Peggy snapped back irritably and then asked, "why not?"

"Well, they're not the only kids in school."

"Maybe not, but at least they're friendly."

"Other kids are too. Even Janet when you get to know her."

"I don't want to know her, thanks."

"That's not a very nice thing to say." Jane's voice sounded very preachy and rubbed Peggy the wrong way.

She knew she shouldn't keep the argument going but did anyway.

"I like Sally. In fact she's invited me over to her house next weekend. She wants me to go home with her Friday right after the program. She's having a slumber party. Especially for me."

Jane shrugged. "OK. But I bet you won't like it."

"Bet I will," Peggy answered obstinately. Actually she had had a nagging doubt about it when Sally had told her who else was being invited, because a couple of them were girls she had thought of as being sort of wild. But she *did* like Sally—and now all the more because of Jane's criticism.

Peggy was keyed up the night of the festival. Aunt Emily had sent her shopping with Miss Murphy the day before. She had said a new dress was a necessity since Peggy had helped to make the festival a success.

The excitement of the evening, the delight in knowing she really looked super in the lemon-yellow dress, gave her a glow that even Aunt Emily noticed. *I am Cinderella going to the ball after all,* she thought as she went downstairs, where her aunt looked at her critically before saying, "Very nice indeed."

Everything went off well, and the program was enthusiastically received by the audience. Peggy was as flushed and excited as though she had personally been the star of the performance. It was so *good* to be a part of the group, to feel as though she really belonged. She had never expected to feel that way out here.

"Hello, Peggy." At the sound of her name spoken behind her she whirled around.

"Mrs. Tremont! Hello. I want you to meet my aunt and uncle." She introduced them, and they chatted for a moment until Mrs. Ferguson paused beside them.

"Lucy, Janet did so well," Aunt Emily said. Mrs. Tremont waited until Mrs. Ferguson had agreed indifferently and then introduced herself.

"I'm Janet's gym teacher." She smiled and held out her hand.

"Oh!" The response was one of startled amazement. Then, with the rudeness Peggy had noticed the evening they had had dinner together, Mrs. Ferguson went on. "From what Janet has said about you, I would have expected someone old and homely. Isn't that what the expression *battle-ax* means?" She smiled as she spoke, but only with her lips.

Peggy could hardly believe her ears and looked at Aunt Emily. Was this an example of the polite society manners her aunt had lectured her about all year? She was glad to see Aunt Emily looked upset too, but Mrs. Tremont only laughed without a trace of resentment.

"There are usually quite a few battle-axes in a school. I remember some from my own experience. Janet *did* do well tonight." And with a friendly nod she moved on.

Sally grabbed Peggy's arm from the other side. "Ready? My folks are waiting over there."

"Yes, I'm ready. You know my aunt and uncle, don't you?"

"Hi." Sally nodded at them. Ordinarily Peggy would have expected her aunt to resent such an offhand greeting, but at least Sally hadn't been rude the way Mrs. Ferguson had been.

"Have a good time, Peggy. Roger will come for you late Sunday afternoon." Her aunt nodded across the room at Sally's parents as she spoke, and Peggy smiled good-bye to her and Jane.

She followed Sally through the crowd of people still milling around in the auditorium to where her parents waited near the door. Peggy liked them at once. Mr. Sanders was big, hearty, and outdoorish looking, and his wife was very friendly. They both smiled at Peggy in reply to the breezy introduction Sally gave. "This is Peggy. Peggy, my folks."

Sally's three younger sisters were in the car, and they and Sally kept such a lively conversation going Peggy didn't have to talk. The uninhibited atmosphere was like a tonic to her after the months of reserve in Aunt Emily's home. She found herself joining in the shrieks of laughter that followed the most ordinary comment, but with the subconscious feeling that her aunt was hovering at her elbow, frowning at the hilarity.

It was fun all the next day. Sally and her three sisters were like steps in a staircase and did everything together. Even before breakfast that morning they played a fast game of badminton in the huge back yard, with each one taking a turn at keeping score. The breakfast table was set on the large screened back porch and glowed in the sunlight streaming in through the bamboo curtains. The girls sat down breathless, the youngest clamoring for pancakes, which promptly appeared.

"Hope you like them, Peggy," Sally said as she rescued the platter from her sisters and passed it to her first. "Take a lot while you have the chance," she urged. "The little monsters can wait for the next batch."

"What an awful thing to say!" Peggy protested.

"What? Monsters? Oh, that's just a term of affection!"

"Call us anything you want, only pass the food," one of them begged.

Syrup, butter, and jelly made the rounds, with Peggy waiting for a signal whether there was to be any prayer offered. She fussed a minute with her napkin, prayed a silent word or two, and picked up her juice.

"Hurry up," one of the girls urged. "We're ready for more."

The whole day was fast-paced like that. In between

other things Sally filled her in on plans for the slumber party. The list of names she reeled off made Peggy's head swim.

"Where are you going to put everyone?"

"Upstairs. Dad had the attic fixed up last winter so he could get rid of us when we felt like making a racket. It's an ideal setup for a slumber party. Come on, I'll show you."

She led the way upstairs, and Peggy saw what she meant. It *was* ideal and already arranged for the party with mattresses and sleeping bags spread out on the floor at one end of the long room.

"I promised I'd help get the food ready. Dad had an old refrigerator put up here so we wouldn't have to track down to the kitchen for everything whenever we have a party. It's already loaded with pop."

Peggy followed her down to the kitchen and helped make sandwiches. The cook had two large cakes ready, one gooey with thick chocolate frosting, the other with swirls of cherry.

The girls began arriving about eight o'clock, their overnight bags loaded with records and tapes.

Sally's mother came up for a moment, dressed to go out. "Just a couple of rules, girls," she said mildly. "The first is to confine the noise to this room. No running around the halls downstairs. The second, no throwing stuff around—cans, brushes, shoes. Sally, you're responsible. Have fun." She paused on her way out the door and smiled over her shoulder at them. "Oh, yes, one more thing. No talking about anyone who isn't here."

She ducked out at the chorus of boos and laughter.

Peggy had listened to the introductions Sally gave. "Girls, you know Peggy, don't you? This is Karen, Diane, Lois, Sue, Janice, Mary, Evie, and Ruth." The names were rattled off so quickly she couldn't keep track of which belonged to which. It wasn't really necessary anyway because there were so much confusion, giggling, and talking going on nobody paid any attention to names.

As the evening went on Peggy began to feel more and more uncomfortable. Everyone was friendly enough, especially Sally, who remembered that Peggy was her special guest. But somehow she felt as though she didn't fit in with this bunch. At first the talk had been general about school and teachers. But it went from there to movie stars and then to boys in general and finally to a few in particular.

Diane was the one who had been out on the most dates though a couple of others had, too, a few times. Even Sally, who frankly said she had only had one real date, entered into the discussion as to what was the accepted thing to say and do on a date. Then Diane began to tell stories she had heard that made Peggy feel embarrassed, ashamed, and very uncomfortable. She glanced around the group as they sat listening and wondered if anyone else felt the way she did. Sally met her eyes and looked embarrassed too. As soon as Diane finished one story, Sally jumped up. "Come on, kids. Let's play records."

There was a scramble for the record cabinet, and both Lois and Diane grabbed for the same one. "Let's do this one," Diane said. "We can dance to it." She started the record player, and the music blasted out.

Peggy felt herself in the way as the other girls began moving in time to the loud beat, snapping their fingers and swaying from side to side. She watched, fascinated. She had not been to any school parties at home since starting junior high, and the parties she had gone to at church had been skating or game nights.

She had seen ads for movies on TV with dancing like this, and they always reminded her of a cultural program she had once seen about a primitive tribe. The anthropologist doing the review had shown scenes of villages having celebrations. The frenzied leaping of the people had stuck in her mind. Now, watching the intensity of the faces of Diane and Lois and even Sally as they jerked and swayed, she was reminded of the scene.

As she stood by the table watching, Sally danced toward her, beckoning. "Come on."

She shook her head. "I don't know how."

Sally stopped. "Come on. I'll teach you. It's easy."

Peggy felt trapped. How could she explain on the spur of the moment that she would feel like a savage in the jungle if she jerked around like that? That would be criticizing Sally's party.

"Look, don't bother about me. I'll look at a magazine or something."

"How about getting out some of the food? I'll be there to help in a minute." Sally was grabbed and whirled away, her face flushed with laughter.

Peggy felt clumsy as she pulled out paper plates and cans of soft drink. The clumsiness was not in what her hands were doing, but in her mind and mouth. She should have had words ready to tell Sally why she didn't want to dance. It was too late to wait until she needed those words. But—if Sally asked questions later, would she know what to answer?

11

The door opening the next morning wakened Peggy because she was sleeping nearest to it. She blinked her eyes sleepily in the light coming in through the open doorway and peered up at the giggling figure standing beside her.

"Hi, Peggy," one of Sally's sisters whispered. "Boy, do you kids look crummy! You look as though you'd been up all night."

"We *were* just about." Peggy yawned. "What time is it, anyhow?"

"About eleven-thirty. The cook said to tell those who want any breakfast to be ready in fifteen minutes 'cause she has to get it out of the way in time for dinner."

"Is it that late?" Peggy exclaimed. "Usually we're in church now."

"Do you go to church?"

"Umhm. Don't you?"

"We've never gone. Except once when our aunt was married, and it was in a church."

Peggy looked at the impish little face grinning down at her and felt sorry for her because of what she was missing.

The girl next to her stirred, sat up, and looked groggily around and then fell back onto the pillow. "Go 'way," she muttered. "It can't be time to get up yet."

The two other sisters poked their heads in just in time

to hear her. They looked at one another, and then all three put their heads together and yelled. "Breakfast!"

The ear-splitting shriek yanked everyone up, and Sally muttered through clenched teeth, "Wait'll I get my hands on those little monsters. And I do mean monsters!" Then she yawned, stretched, and got up. "That's probably absolutely the last call we'll get, so we'd better get down there but fast."

"Yipes! It's almost twelve, and my dad is coming for me at twelve-thirty," Diane groaned. "We've got a big affair on this afternoon, and I'm supposed to go home and look pleasant. I feel about as pleasant as a porcupine right now."

"Is that different from usual?" Sally asked, teasing. Peggy turned her head to hide a smile. She couldn't think of anyone who was more of a pill than Diane except Janet Ferguson—and Jane the way she used to be.

The next hour was a mad scramble as everyone tried to eat breakfast, gather up stuff, and get dressed between groans of tiredness.

"You all asked for it," Sally's mother remarked unsympathetically. "Next time get to sleep earlier."

"Mother!" Sally exclaimed. "Don't be so juvenile."

When the last car had gone, Sally sank down in a big chair in the living room with a deep sigh. "I'm beat. Absolutely beat!"

"Me too."

"What time did you get to sleep?" Sally yawned.

"The last time I remember looking at my watch it was three-thirty. How about you?"

"I think it was four when Diane finally quit yapping in my ear."

A sister appeared in the doorway. "Mother says you've got to get this place cleaned up. And quick, before dinner."

"OK, OK! Now run along, little girl scout, and leave us alone."

"She said *quick*."

"—ly."

"Huh?"

"Oh, never mind!. Why I bother to correct your grammar I'll never know."

Peggy laughed as the pigtails disappeared. "She's cute."

"Yeah. If she's somebody else's sister."

"No, really she is. So are the other two."

"Oh, I guess so," Sally admitted. "We do have fun most of the time. Though I wouldn't let them know it."

"Know what?" The question came from the doorway.

"Hey, are you here again?"

"Mother said you were to be quick, and you haven't even started."

"Beat it, pest! Be right back, Peggy."

"I'll come help."

"You shouldn't have to. You're a guest."

"I helped make the mess," Peggy replied, following Sally upstairs.

"Ugh! It *is* a mess." Sally wrinkled her nose at the empty softdrink cans, the crumpled napkins, the cake crumbs, and the smears of lipstick and mascara on the pillow cases and towels. "My father sometimes says civilized people can act like pigs. He'd sure say that if he could see this place. My mother never lets him come up after I've had kids sleep over until it gets cleaned up."

"Do you want the blankets folded up? And where do I put the wet towels?"

"Just dump everything in the shower stall out of sight. Mom will have the cleaning woman finish the rest tomorrow, if we get the worst of the mess cleaned up. We'll have to hurry to get that much done before time for dinner."

Peggy rolled up sleeping bags and looked around as Sally said, "How come you never learned to dance?" Then, not waiting for an answer, she said, "Of course, what we were doing isn't really dancing, to hear my grandmother. She claims you only have to know how to wiggle around in time to the music."

This time she did wait for an answer, and Peggy said, "You know what you just said that your dad said—about civilized people acting like pigs? Well, sometimes civilized people look like uncivilized people. If you just saw pictures of people jerking around like that and didn't hear the music, and didn't have any idea what they were doing, wouldn't you think they were crazy?"

Sally frowned. "Yeah, I never thought of that. You're right. I bet it does look dumb. Next time I'll have everyone look in the mirror." She grinned at Peggy.

Peggy didn't smile back because words and music were running through her mind. "I have decided to follow Jesus. . . . Though none go with me, still I will follow. . . ."

She tried to keep her voice just as ordinary sounding as when she talked about anything else as she said, "I just think it looks as though you're not in control of yourself. And if you're not in control of yourself, the only person who should control you is God."

"I get it. You're talking about religion, and it's against your religion to dance." Sally was as matter-of-fact about this as she seemed to be about everything. Somehow this gave Peggy a confidence she wouldn't have had if Sally had been more curious or had laughed.

"It isn't only religion, Sally." She groped for the right words. "It's believing in Someone. There are lots of religions, but only one that is true. That's Christianity. Jesus was a real person who really lived and then died and rose again to take away our sins and keep us from wanting to do wrong things anymore." She went on

94

earnestly, hoping she was making sense to Sally. "The Bible says, 'For God so loved the world that He gave His only begotten Son, that whoever believes in Him should not perish but have everlasting life.'"

Sally looked at her thoughtfully for a moment and then brushed off the subject with a careless shrug. "You're funny, Peggy. You're so serious about things. But I like you because of that. We'll have to get better acquainted this summer so we're good friends by next year."

"Oh, I won't be here next year."

"How come?"

"I'm only visiting here for this one year. The Conways are my aunt and uncle."

"I didn't know that! Where do you live?"

"Pennsylvania."

"Oh, phooey! I wish you did live here."

"I don't," Peggy answered honestly. "Oh, it's OK!" she added hastily. "But it isn't home. You know how it would be if you had to live somewhere else. Just think how you would miss your sisters."

"Yeah!" Sally agreed eloquently. "Some miss!"

The middle sister poked her head into the room. "Dinner's ready, you two. Hurry up. All I've done today is chase you around, Sally."

"Quit then," was the unsympathetic reply.

"Smells wonderful," Peggy exclaimed and followed them downstairs.

It was almost five before Roger came for her. After saying good-bye to Sally's parents, she looked for the sisters.

"I think they went swimming," Sally said.

"Say good-bye to them for me. They're cute. And thanks, Sally, for everything. I had a good time even though I'm dead on my feet."

"Me, too! Hope I have enough sense to go to bed early tonight. See you in math. It was fun having you."

They walked toward the car slowly, and Jane stuck her head out the window. "Hurry up, slowpoke."

"Hi, Jane." Peggy stumbled into the car feeling as though her legs were made of lead. Her head felt funny, and her eyelids prickly with the effort she had to make to keep them open.

"Don't ask me anything that requires any thinking," she mumbled, leaning her head against the back of the seat. "I don't think I could even add two and two right now and get an answer."

"Then you don't want to read your letter?"

After a moment the words penetrated Peggy's consciousness, and she opened her eyes and sat up straight. "What letter? Isn't this Sunday?" she asked fuzzily.

"It's a special delivery. Came just after we got home from church so I brought it along. But I didn't know you wouldn't be able to read it," she said with mock sympathy.

Peggy snatched it, glanced at the handwriting and return address and said, "From Ann. I thought it would be from Mother and Dad. Now why would she send a special delivery?"

"Well, open it and find out," Jane urged impatiently. "Special deliveries are usually sort of important, aren't they?"

Peggy tore the envelope open and scanned the letter, excitedly reading it aloud in snatches. "Writing to tell you we're coming to California for our vacation ... relatives not far from where you are ... Dad is preaching ... coming home July 30 ... if you want a ride...."

"Oh, good!" she beamed at Jane, her tiredness forgotten in this breath from home. "Here, you can read it." She handed over the letter, remembering that not many months ago she would never have shared with Jane a letter from anyone at home.

"She sounds nice." Jane handed the letter back. "I've been wondering when you were going to leave," she added, looking out the window.

Peggy looked at her quickly. Was that regret in her voice because Peggy was going home? Or regret that she would be staying almost a month longer than the original plan?

"I'll have to ask Aunt Emily if it's all right with her if I stay," she said anxiously.

"She won't care. It'll only be a month longer."

The words decided Peggy. That was it. Jane was sorry she was staying on.

"I can write them that I don't want to wait," she began stiffly but was too tired to continue without breaking down in tears. As she stared away from Jane and out through the window, she was reminded of a frequent remark her mother made. "Never make an important decision when you're tired," and she said out loud, "Maybe I'll stay and maybe I won't."

But the decision was taken out of her hands the next morning. Aunt Emily stopped her as she was dashing out to where Roger waited with the car.

"Peggy, I had a letter from your mother Saturday asking if you could stay a month longer." She stopped as Peggy nodded. "Is that what your letter yesterday was about?"

Peggy nodded again, and her aunt went on, "If you're willing to wait, it would save the expense of your ticket home."

Peggy hadn't thought about saving her parents the money for plane fare and was ashamed for being so self-centered. So she forced a smile. "If you don't mind my being here—"

"A few more weeks won't matter. It may be the last time we see you. I'll write your mother, and you can get more definite word as to when your friends will be here. Run along now so you won't be late."

Peggy walked out and down the steps, scolding herself. Why did she automatically interpret everything Jane and her aunt said in the wrong way? She acted as though they hated having her here. She didn't think Jane, at least, felt that way.

I won't be like that anymore, she decided and climbed into the car beside Jane with a bright, "Hi! Sorry I'm late."

12

The end of the school year came quickly and happily. Peggy couldn't help contrasting it with last June, when she had dreaded vacation because it meant coming to California. As she thought back over the year, she had to smile at the foolish fears and anxieties that had gnawed at her. She had so dreaded living with Aunt Emily, but in the months she had been here they had had very little contact. And what they had had was mostly in her favor. Her eyes wandered to her clothes closet, stuffed with clothes that were gifts from her aunt.

She ticked off on her fingers the things she had gained during the year. New clothes, an understanding and friendship with Jane, more self-confidence, friendships with Lisa and Mrs. Tremont. But another, sobering thought came. What had she *given* to anyone during the year? Lisa's salvation? Not really, because that had mainly come about through books Lisa had read. Sally hadn't paid any attention to what she had told her. She had got no place with Jane in talking about being a Christian. There wasn't one thing she could honestly say she had done to help anyone.

"Shame on you!" she scolded accusingly. "It's terrible to be so absolutely useless when you know how necessary it is for people to know about the Lord Jesus."

She had been praying every day for Uncle Walter

especially but hadn't seen any results. And then in early June he went on a camping trip with Mr. Ferguson.

When Peggy first heard about it she almost exploded with laughter at the thought of her uncle out camping. She tried to picture him building a fire dressed in his beautifully pressed suit and white shirt with the onyx cuff links. As it turned out he didn't wear a business suit. But he still looked like a dignified businessman in the camping clothes that had been tailored to him.

Peggy remembered the few times her dad had gone on fishing trips, and the memory of his tall lean figure in the patched hunting jacket and old whipcord trousers made her throat choke up. How *wonderful* it would be to see him again!

She and Jane were just coming back from a badminton game when Mr. Ferguson drove up in his station wagon. He waved at them and leaned to open the door for Roger to put in Uncle Walter's fishing gear and bags.

When they were ready to leave, Mr. Ferguson waved again and called, "'Bye, kids," with his easy, friendly grin. Their uncle ducked his head in their direction with a tight little smile.

What will they do together all the time? Peggy wondered as she watched the car pull away. *They're so different, and Uncle Walter finds it so hard to talk to people.*

Then as she followed Jane down to the family room another thought struck her. Maybe this camping trip was Mr. Ferguson's idea to get a chance to really talk to Uncle Walter. And maybe Uncle Walter was willing to go, knowing how changed Mr. Ferguson was, because he was really interested in these new ideas. Her pulse quickened at the new possibilities that were opening up. A week was a long time, and a lot could be accomplished.

So intent was she on these thoughts and so far away

in her imagination, it was difficult for even the sharpened impatience of Jane's voice to penetrate.

"What did you say?" Peggy looked at her blankly.

"Nothing important. You were miles away, I guess."

"Yes, I was with Uncle Walter on his trip." She answered without thinking and only realized what she had said when Jane exclaimed, "What? What do you mean?"

Peggy laughed. "That did sound funny, didn't it? I only meant I was thinking about them."

"Why?" Jane's voice sounded casual enough on the surface, but Peggy thought she detected a current of interest underneath. She almost had the feeling that Jane knew what she was thinking.

With a feeling of breathless daring she replied, "Since Mr. Ferguson is a Christian, he'll be talking to Uncle Walter while they're together, and maybe he'll be saved."

There was silence in the room when she finished. Complete silence. And then Jane broke into a storm of tears. She buried her head in her arms as she sat at the soda fountain counter and cried with deep, shuddering sobs.

Peggy stared at her, not knowing what to do or say. Then as she started toward her, the laundry door was shoved open and Mrs. Vanacek and Lisa looked in.

"Peggy! What's wrong?" Lisa stopped as she saw Jane, who seemed not to notice anyone. Then Lisa walked swiftly over and sat down on the stool next to Jane, putting her arm around her shoulder gently. She didn't try to talk but merely sat quietly, patting Jane's shoulders comfortingly. Presently the tears became quieter, and Jane fumbled in the pockets of her shorts for a Kleenex.

"Here's a clean one," Lisa said quickly. Jane took it, wiped her eyes, and blew her nose. Then she brushed her hair back from her face and sat up straight. Without looking at either Peggy or Lisa she slid off the stool and said, her voice thick, "I'm going upstairs. Don't come with me."

They listened to the door close behind her at the top of the stairs. Peggy said with an anxious frown, "I wonder what's the matter? All of a sudden she burst into tears, for no reason at all."

"Maybe she doesn't feel well."

"She was all right until now. We were just out playing badminton and came in and were talking and everything was OK. Maybe I should go up with her," she questioned uncertainly.

"I wouldn't," Lisa said quickly. "Give her some time by herself."

"Maybe you're right." Then she turned with a smile. "How are you? It's been so long since we talked."

"I know," Lisa said a trifle wistfully. Then her expressive mouth curved into a smile and she added, "Everything is wonderful. We have such good young people's meetings in the church I go to. The sponsors are super. I even teach a Sunday school class of darling little five-year-old kids."

"I'm glad. I know how much I was helped by the people in the church I went to after I was saved."

"It's sort of funny the way I found out about the church. I was looking at the paper one day, and I saw an ad for someone to do part-time cleaning. That's something I practically grew up on," she said with a laugh. "So I decided if it didn't take too much time, maybe I could get the job. It's really easy because it's just a couple with no children, so nothing gets very dirty. Well, it turned out they are Christians, and they asked if I went to church anyplace, and I told them I had just been saved. So they invited me to their church, and they are the sponsors of the youth group that meets every week and on Sunday."

Peggy had been only half-listening as she watched

Lisa's expressive face and thought how pretty she was. *I wish I looked like her,* she thought wistfully and enviously. Then the name Lisa mentioned brought her attention back abruptly.

"Who did you say?"

"Mrs. Tremont. She teaches school—"

"I know!" Peggy broke in excitedly. "I have her. I mean, she's my gym teacher. She is wonderful! To think we both know her!"

They smiled at one another companionably, and Peggy felt a surge of regret that going home meant not seeing Lisa anymore. The thought brought the reminder that she wasn't supposed to be talking to her now, and she explained to Lisa.

"You know how my aunt is," she finished apologetically with a shrug of her shoulders. "It isn't that she's mean on purpose or anything like that. It's just the way she was brought up, I guess."

"I know. I'm used to it, but Mother is very sensitive about it. I think when she first started working like this, more people felt the way your aunt does, and Mother thinks everyone still does. If she were a Christian it would make a difference." She gave a small sigh as she added, "Sometimes I get awfully discouraged, Peggy. About my father, I mean."

"He still—I mean, he hasn't stopped—"

"No. He wasn't even home all weekend." Lisa's voice was small and ashamed. Peggy reached out quickly and put her hand over Lisa's, which were clasped in a tight fist in her lap.

"I'm going to pray about him too," she promised earnestly. "I can't do anything else. I've been doing that about my uncle, and this week he went on a camping trip with a friend of his who is saved, and I just know this man will talk to him."

"If only some of Dad's friends would be saved it would be easier. He won't listen to me. He thinks I'm criticizing *him* or sassing him back. He can't see that I love him."

The conversation brought Peggy's thoughts back to Jane. "That's when Jane started crying," she said thoughtfully. "When I said something to her about Uncle Walter being saved."

"Maybe she thinks she doesn't want him to be any different," Lisa guessed.

"Maybe. But she doesn't usually cry about things. I'm the one who bursts into tears for no reason at all, not Jane." She stood up. "I'd better go see if she's all right."

"Will your aunt be mad because you came down?"

"No, because I didn't do it on purpose to see you. I'm going to be here for about a month so I'll see you again. I'll *make* my aunt let us talk for a real long time before I go."

"I wish I could ask you to come over to my house. But I don't suppose your aunt would let you. and maybe you wouldn't want to."

"Of course I would," Peggy answered indignantly. "If your mother will let me come, I'll ask my aunt." She turned to go upstairs and then remembered something. "Hey, I forgot to tell you! Ann Parker and her folks are coming out here for a vacation next month, and I'm going to ride home with them. I know she'll want to meet you."

"And I want to meet her," Lisa answered eagerly.

"Maybe we could go to your house while she is here. My aunt can't say no, if her folks say yes. At least, not so easily."

"Wonderful!" Lisa answered, and then turned toward the laundry as her mother called.

Jane's door was closed when Peggy got upstairs, and the stereo blared with one of Jane's favorite numbers.

She decided to knock anyway. There was no answer even though she tried several times. It was just like it had been when she first came here a year ago.

Finally she turned regretfully away. The fragile friendship they had built so slowly over the long year was lost, and all because of something she had unwittingly said.

"If I only knew what it was!" she muttered, opening her door. As she did so she heard Jane's door open and turned to see Jane peeking out.

"Can I come in a minute?" she asked eagerly.

Jane shook her head. "Not now. I don't want to talk. But I wanted to tell you I'm not mad at you about anything." She closed the door again firmly, but this time Peggy didn't mind. They were still friends.

She kept her promise to Lisa and all week prayed hard for her father and Uncle Walter. She didn't put it into words even to herself, but she couldn't help feeling that there was more chance for Lisa's father to be saved than her uncle.

Then Uncle Walter came home. Aunt Emily had gone out, and Peggy was sitting with Jane on the edge of the swimming pool when the car swung around to the side entrance. He and Mr. Ferguson sat in the car for quite a while talking after they pulled into the driveway. Mr. Ferguson gestured emphatically as he spoke, and Peggy could see her uncle nodding agreement. Finally they got out and began to unload the car. Then the two men strolled over to the pool.

"Hi, girls." Mr. Ferguson grinned down at them. "I brought the boss back safe and sound."

It was then that Peggy, eager for an answer to her prayers, looked up at her uncle and sensed a difference in him. She thought a person would have to be blind and deaf not to notice it. Not that he looked different exactly. He just *was* different. The reserved manner that much a part of him was still evident, but the coldness was gone. She didn't dare look at Jane to see if she could see it too. Jane hadn't even answered her uncle's greeting, but only looked up at him wordlessly.

Then Mr. Ferguson clapped him on the shoulder. "I'd better be going. My family will think I've left them for good."

Uncle Walter turned and walked back to the car with him. "Thanks again, Jim," the girls heard him say, and Mr. Ferguson answered, "Don't thank me. Thank God."

Jane caught her breath and stared at Peggy. "What will Mother say?" she whispered, real fright showing in her voice. Then she picked up her towel, jumped up, and hurried toward the house.

With a troubled frown Peggy watched her go. That was a disquieting thought. Would she try to talk or laugh Uncle Walter out of his new-found faith? She was such a dominant person, maybe he wouldn't be able to stand up to her about this.

What her uncle said to Aunt Emily, Peggy never knew. And if her aunt was upset, no one knew that either. She didn't show any outward sign of inner turmoil as she sat erectly at the dinner table that evening, giving orders to the maid in her usual manner. Peggy was sure that nothing could induce her aunt to show emotion in front of anyone else, especially in front of the servants.

There was one very awkward moment at the beginning of the meal just after the maid had served the first course and gone back to the kitchen. Aunt Emily had given the signal to begin eating by picking up her fork, when Uncle Walter cleared his throat and said gruffly, "We'll say a prayer before we eat."

As his wife looked at him in amazement, he bowed his head and said quickly, "For what we are about to receive, we thank You. Amen."

It was over so quickly and had been so unexpected, Peggy hadn't had time to bow her head. She saw the maid come back with the hot rolls and stare in surprise at the scene. Peggy was sure this bothered Aunt Emily more than anything else, but she only tightened her lips and said nothing. Undoubtedly she was thinking of the talk that would go on in the kitchen when the maid reported back what she had seen.

Peggy wanted to say something to her uncle after dinner but was afraid to with her aunt listening. So she set her alarm that night to be sure to be up when Uncle Walter left for the office. It wasn't until she started down the stairs that she remembered that Jane got up to eat breakfast with Uncle Walter. She hung over the railing, listening for the sound of voices. When she didn't hear anything, she tiptoed downstairs, across the hall, and out the front door.

When Uncle Walter came out she said shyly, "I wanted to tell you I'm glad. About what's happened to you, I mean."

He looked embarrassed, and for a minute she was sorry she had said anything. Then he gave a brief smile. "Thank you. I have a great deal to learn. I don't expect it will be very easy." He looked at her. "You are a Christian too?" When she nodded he said, "You know all about it then. I wish I had known sooner."

He got in the car, settled back, and Roger drove off. Peggy looked after it, ashamed, a lump in her throat. All year she had lived under her uncle's roof, sat at meals with him, and he hadn't known she was a Christian. Even if she could never have been the one to bring him to the Lord, at least she ought to have spoken of Christ to him.

She turned to go in. If a person could only know in advance how things would turn out, it would be easier to say and do the right things at the right time. What could she do in the brief time that was left?

13

There wasn't much chance for anything. The last week slipped by so rapidly that Peggy was afraid she wouldn't be ready when the Parkers came for her. She finally got around to begin sorting out all the things she had accumulated, with Jane watching and offering advice.

"I'm afraid there won't be room for all this stuff," Peggy worried, sitting back on her heels and looking at it. "They'll have so much of their own in the car already."

"What did you save this for?" Jane picked up a napkin with a large red bow pinned to it.

"It's a souvenir of our home room party. I'm keeping it to remind me of all the kids. I'm going to put everything like that in a big scrapbook I have at home."

"I wouldn't think you'd want to remember some things from being out here." Jane had her back turned so that Peggy, looking up from where she squatted on the floor, couldn't see her face.

"That's what I thought at first," she answered frankly. "I thought I simply couldn't stand being here. But, you know, it's a funny thing. When I look back on the year, I can see I've had a lot of fun."

"I wish you could stay here always." Jane's voice was so low Peggy wasn't sure she had heard correctly.

"Do you really mean that?" Peggy jumped up and walked around to stand in front of her sister.

"Of course. I wouldn't say it if I didn't."

"Maybe you just think so because I'm going. Maybe it would be different if I did stay here all the time."

"It's going to be lonesome for me," Jane answered with her old pouty expression. "I'll have to go to school all by myself, and you'll have Bill and all your friends."

"I'll have to get used to walking again." Peggy laughed, trying to get Jane into a happier mood.

"You'll probably forget all about me."

"No, I won't," Peggy protested earnestly. "I'll write you real often. And maybe you can come and visit at Christmas again. And next summer too."

Jane shrugged and changed the subject without answering directly.

As each day brought her return home closer Peggy grew more and more excited. Aunt Emily had solved the problem of packing by suggesting that Miss Murphy could express home whatever could not be squeezed into the Parker car.

Ann had written again, this time giving more details of their plans, and Peggy waited impatiently for the day they would arrive. She was up early that morning and gulped a quick breakfast, not knowing just what time they would come.

She went outside and walked up and down the driveway, wishing Jane were there to help share the excitement. But when she had urged Jane to wait with her, she had shaken her head.

"I promised Stella I'd come over."

"Not today, Jane. Please! I want you to be here to meet them."

But Jane had shaken her head stubbornly again, and Peggy knew it was no use to argue. If Jane had her mind made up, it would take a miracle to change it.

She was watching for the familiar green car she had ridden in so many times to church and was quite unprepared for the flashy new red and white car that turned slowly into the drive as though not sure of where it was going. She stood looking for a moment to be sure it was not someone coming to see her aunt, and then ran down the driveway quickly as she recognized Ann waving frantically out the back window.

The car had barely stopped before the door flew open and Ann burst out. "Peggy! You look wonderful! I can't believe it's you!"

"If I were Peggy I'd resent that." Mrs. Parker smiled as she got out and hugged her. "It's so good to see you again."

"Hi, Mrs. Parker. If you keep this up, you'll have me thinking no one will recognize me. Hello, Mr. Parker." She bent down to see who else was in the car.

"Remember me? I'm Jim. I'm sure I haven't changed." Ann's younger brother got out of the car as he spoke and stretched. Then he looked around and whistled. "Some place they've got here."

"It's beautiful," Ann agreed appreciatively. "You'll hate to leave."

"Oh, no!" Peggy replied emphatically. "I can't wait to get home. Come in and meet my aunt. Jane isn't here, and Uncle Walter is at the office, but I'm sure my aunt is home."

"We can stay only a few minutes," Mr. Parker replied. "We have a dozen or more friends who have to be looked up in the next two days. We'll come in now, and then not be back again until early Wednesday to pick you up. Will you be ready?"

"I'm ready right now," Peggy answered happily.

She led the way through the wide front door. As they stepped into the spacious hall, Miss Murphy came out of the living room.

"Is Aunt Emily busy?"

"She's telephoning just now. She asked me to tell you to wait in here until she's through."

"Miss Murphy, this is Mr. and Mrs. Parker and Ann and Jim."

"I'm glad to meet you." Miss Murphy smiled. "I understand you'll be taking Peggy away in a few days."

"Yes, her parents can't wait to get her home."

Miss Murphy smiled politely and excused herself.

"She's Aunt Emily's secretary," Peggy whispered in answer to the question on Ann's face. "She's nice, but very businesslike. I guess that's why my aunt likes her so much."

"How could you ever get used to this?" Ann looked around at the thick rugs and rich draperies of the living room.

Peggy looked around too. "It's funny," she said thoughtfully. "I hadn't realized how used I am to it. I hardly notice how expensive things are now, the way I did at first."

Aunt Emily came in then, acknowledged Peggy's introductions in her gracious but remote manner, and asked polite questions about their trip.

"Do you have a place to stay while you're here?"

Peggy thought she was just making sure they didn't expect to stay there.

But Mrs. Parker answered, "Yes, we have a number of friends who are planning for our visit."

"I thought if it is agreeable with you, your daughter could stay here with Peggy if she wouldn't mind sharing a room."

"Oh, wonderful!" Peggy exclaimed with shining eyes. She had planned to ask if Ann could stay one night, but she hadn't dared ask for the whole time.

Mrs. Parker laughed. "It might be a good idea to let

them get some of their talking done before we start home. Otherwise I'm not sure we could stand the chatter. Thank you for the invitation."

Peggy gave a little inward sigh of relief. Aunt Emily apparently approved of their appearance, or she never would have given the invitation. They somehow didn't even look as though they had been traveling for several weeks. She smiled around at them mistily. They were *so* nice!

Aunt Emily stood up. "I must go. My calendar is so full this week that my time isn't my own. Perhaps I will see you when you come for Peggy?"

"We hope to get an early start, but we certainly don't want to disrupt your household schedule," Mr. Parker answered.

"That won't matter. The servants will be up by six, so there will be someone to help you put things in the car. I shall probably not see you then, so I shall say good-bye now." She turned to Peggy. "You may entertain your friend as you like," and she was gone.

There was silence for a moment, and Peggy didn't know whether to explain that that was just her aunt's way or not say anything at all.

But Ann said, "I never expected to get to stay with you, Peggy. I'm glad because I've got so much to tell you."

"Jim, get Ann's suitcase from the car while I jot down the phone number here in case we need to get in touch with her. Then we must be on our way."

After they had gone, Peggy took Ann up to her room and waited while she unpacked the few things she needed for the short visit. Then she took her on a tour of the grounds and laughed at the typically Ann exclamations of delight.

"I hope we get to try that pool."

"Let's do it tomorrow when Jane's here."

113

"When will she be home?"

"Sometime before dinner. I think she went away on purpose so she wouldn't be here when you first came."

It was while they were in the rec room having a game of table tennis that Ann asked about Lisa.

"She'll be here tomorrow," Peggy answered. "Tuesday is the regular day for her mother to come, and she's been helping since school was out." After a moment's hesitation she found herself telling Ann all about her aunt's refusal to let her talk to Lisa and the reason for it. "But the last time I talked to Lisa, I told her you were coming, and of course she wants to see you. She wants us to come to her house, but I don't know if Aunt Emily will allow it."

"Does Lisa really look like her picture?"

"I've never seen a picture of her, but she's beautiful. I mean really beautiful."

"In her picture she looks—oh, I don't know—glamorous is the only word I can think of."

Peggy frowned. "Maybe that would be the right word if she weren't a Christian. She doesn't try to look glamorous, I'm sure."

"Have you heard from Alice much?" Ann asked then, casually.

"Not lately. We wrote a lot at first but then not so much later. Why?"

"I'm not exactly sure what to tell you about her. She's been—different lately."

"How? Does she ever come to church?"

"She did a few times. With Dan."

"With Dan? You mean, like a date?"

"Uh-huh."

"But she didn't used to like him!" Peggy exclaimed. "She was sort of snobbish about it. I remember how mad

I got at her because she thought it was so funny his dad was only a janitor."

Ann nodded. "I know. But that's part of what I mean. Lately she's been sort of boy crazy. She only came to young people's a couple of times when Dan asked her. But now she's been going other places. With other kids."

Though Ann didn't say definitely, Peggy could tell from the way she sounded that they weren't the right kind of places or kids. "I guess I'd better get home," she said soberly. "Maybe I can help her somehow. She is my very best friend. Or anyway she was."

"I hope she still will be. I hate to see her get in with the wrong bunch at school."

"There are problems everywhere you go, aren't there?" Peggy sighed. "Let me tell you all about things out here this year." They curled up on the sofa and talked until the maid came looking for them for lunch.

"I'm sorry! I forgot to tell you I had a guest," Peggy apologized.

"That's all right. Mrs. Conway told Frances about her. You're going home in a couple of days, I hear. We'll miss you."

"Thank you!" Peggy was surprised and touched by the genuine feeling in the maid's voice.

When Jane came home later in the day, she was cool and distant in her attitude, and Peggy looked at Ann with a "see what I mean?" expression. She particularly resented the way Jane stared at Ann, so obviously seeing her limp. But Ann ignored the way she acted and included her in everything that was said. Peggy found herself gradually relaxing as she realized that Jane was thawing a little.

When they went to bed that evening, Peggy was sure Jane felt left out. But though both she and Ann urged

115

her to come in and talk, Jane refused with a curt, "No thanks. I won't know anyone you talk about."

They swam in the pool the next morning with Ann showing Jane some new strokes.

"Where did you learn to swim like that?" Jane asked as they climbed out to sit on the edge of the pool in the hot sun. Peggy heard the grudging admiration in her voice.

"In Warm Springs, Georgia." Ann held out her left leg and explained matter-of-factly. "Maybe you didn't know that I had polio even though hardly anyone gets it anymore. When the doctors found it wasn't going to leave me really crippled the way they thought at first, one of the men in our church—you know the Wilsons, Peggy?—sent Mother and me to Warm Springs for a month as a Christmas present. That's where I learned to swim, and it helped strengthen my leg so that I only limp a little bit."

Peggy had heard Ann talk about it only once before, but she had always wondered how she could take her handicap in such an ordinary way. That seemed to be the thing that warmed Jane completely, because her attitude toward Ann changed and she was frankly admiring of her.

The rest of the morning they talked and giggled and ducked each other in the pool and were in high spirits when they went in to lunch. As they finished Ann asked, "Is Lisa here by now? I can't wait to meet her."

Peggy looked at Jane before she answered slowly, "I think so. I'll go ask if we can do down and see her."

Excusing herself, she went through the living room and over to the den. When Miss Murphy answered her knock and opened the door, she stopped just inside and stood waiting anxiously until her aunt looked around.

"Could we go down and see Lisa for a few minutes?" She saw the frown that began to gather on her aunt's forehead and added in a rush, "Ann wants to meet her. They've been writing to each other."

After a moment with a gesture of resignation, Aunt Emily said, "Oh, very well!" and Peggy dashed out before she could change her mind.

"Let's hurry," she said, bursting into the breakfast room.

As she got up from the table Ann said, "I feel guilty just walking away from these dishes. Shouldn't we offer to help do them?"

"Of course not!" Jane answered and led the way downstairs. The laundry door was standing partway open. Lisa peeked out at the sound of their voices and then came out smiling shyly.

"Hello," she said.

But Ann rushed over and hugged her. "You're just like I thought you'd be, only more so."

"Is that good?" Lisa asked mischievously. Then she turned to Peggy. "I'm sorry. I didn't mean to leave you out. Or you." She turned to Jane.

"Go ahead and talk to Ann. We don't mind," Peggy replied.

Lisa looked anxiously at Peggy. "Do you think you could come to my house for supper tonight?"

Peggy gulped. She'd been saying so bravely that she'd insist on being allowed to go, but now that the actual moment to ask Aunt Emily was facing her, she was scared. She could see Mrs. Vanacek through the open doorway and imagined that her grim expression was daring them to come. She looked at Jane, hoping she would offer to ask, but Jane only tossed a Ping-Pong ball from one hand to the other without meeting her eye.

"I'll go ask," she said weakly and walked slowly upstairs.

"*Please* make her let us go. *Please* make her," she said

117

over and over under her breath as she went through the hall and across the living room to the den. The door was open and her uncle came out, saying over his shoulder, "Jim and I are going for a round of golf."

She waited until he had gone into the hall and then said in a small, timid voice, "Aunt Emily?"

"Yes?"

Peggy swallowed. How *could* she ask?

"Well, what is it, Peggy? I'm very busy."

"We were wondering—that is, Ann and I—the thing is—Lisa has invited us to her house for supper tonight." She waited for the explosion, which came immediately.

"*Absolutely not!*"

There was no recourse from such finality and Peggy turned away. But she was stopped by her uncle's voice. "Why absolutely not?"

"Such a ridiculous idea!" her aunt fumed. "What would make you want to do a thing like that?"

"She invited us," Peggy answered hopefully.

"I don't see why they can't go if they have an invitation." Her uncle's tone was mild, but underneath was a firmness that made Peggy understand why he was considered such a successful businessman.

"Walter! I hardly think it is necessary for you to make an issue out of this! Peggy knows my position on this matter."

"I do not intend to make an issue of it. Peggy, tell her you accept."

She stood helplessly, looking from one to the other. Her aunt was standing rigid with anger. "She goes against my wishes!"

"But with my permission. Those people are all right," her uncle replied. "If they're good enough to clean our clothes, they're good enough to eat with."

Realizing that her aunt was no longer aware of her,

Peggy hurried from the room and dashed downstairs. "We can go!"

"Did she say I could go too?" It was Jane asking, and Peggy looked at Lisa in consternation. She had never thought of including Jane, but Lisa said quickly and positively, "Of course you're coming."

"It wasn't Aunt Emily," Peggy explained. "It was Uncle Walter."

"What?" The amazement in Jane's voice was an expression of Peggy's feelings. But she was also puzzled about Jane's wanting to come.

Now why? she wondered later when she was getting ready to go. *I certainly hope her being along won't spoil everything. It would be just like her to be critical of something and make Mrs. Vanacek mad.*

14

Peggy glanced around nervously as she and Ann and Jane waited for Roger. Surely Aunt Emily wouldn't let them get away with this adventure that she so strongly opposed! But the car came, and they climbed in and were safely on the way. As they went, she filled in the other two on some of the things Lisa had told her about her home so they would have some idea what to expect.

The Vanacek home was on the outskirts of the city in a run-down section. The house itself wasn't bad on the outside except that it was terribly in need of paint. But the small front yard was a mass of flowers, which helped take attention away from the house.

Lisa greeted them at the door and led them inside without a trace of apology.

If it were my house, I'd be embarrassed to death, Peggy thought with a feeling of shame that she should put so much importance on things. But as she looked at the rickety furniture, which had been partially disguised by slipcovers, and at the bare floors, something else impressed her. Everything was so clean. Even Aunt Emily would have to admit that.

The supper was delicious. The proof of this as far as Peggy was concerned was not only how it tasted to her, but the amount Jane ate. After a few half-hearted nibbles of what Lisa had laughingly called her mother's special goulash, a surprised look had crossed Jane's face. Then she had had three helpings. Somehow that helped soften the grim expression Mrs. Vanacek had worn ever since they had come.

Just as they were starting dessert, the front door opened abruptly and staggering footsteps crossed the small living room. They all looked up and stared at the figure swaying in the dining room doorway. In spite of his unkempt, unshaven appearance, anyone would know he was Lisa's father, for she was his image. They had the same deep blue eyes fringed with thick lashes, though his were bloodshot, and the same startling perfect features.

There was complete silence in the room for a moment except for his heavy breathing until Lisa made a small sound and pushed back her chair. But her mother waved her down. "Sit still," she commanded and moved toward her husband.

"Come," she said.

"Gonna join the company," he mumbled, trying to pull away. But she took a firmer grip on his arm and led him toward the kitchen. Lisa's cheeks were flushed, and it was evident the tears were close, for she blinked her long eyelashes rapidly to hold them back.

Then Jane released the tension by saying calmly, "I'd like another helping of—what did you call this?" as though nothing unusual had happened.

Lisa smiled at her gratefully, and after a moment Ann went on with the story she had been telling. Mrs. Vanacek came back just as they finished eating. Ann and Peggy both insisted they should help with dishes, but she refused.

"Lisa won't help either this time," she said firmly. "Anton, you come."

Lisa's eleven-year-old brother, who had sat through the meal without saying a word, now made up for his silence in protests. But his mother simply pointed to the kitchen, and he went.

The girls went into the living room, and when Roger came for them at nine they went reluctantly.

"We've hardly started to get acquainted," Ann protested.

"I know," Lisa agreed tearfully. "And I don't know when I'll ever see you again. Peggy, thanks for everything. Especially for being so nice."

Peggy was near tears herself. "I'll never, never forget you. And I'll write real often."

Lisa went out to the car with them after they had thanked Mrs. Vanacek, who answered them with the first real smile Peggy had ever seen on her face.

As Roger started the motor, Jane leaned across Peggy out the window. "I'll see you around, Lisa," she said casually.

The car pulled away before Lisa could do more than give a startled nod, but Peggy demanded, "Do you really mean that? That you'll be friendly with her when she comes to the house?"

"Sure. Why not?"

"I thought you wouldn't like her. And that you'd be sorry you went. Especially after her dad came in." She shivered. "I was scared of him."

"I wasn't scared," Jane replied. "I've seen people like that before. Once at a party at our house on Christmas, one man was real awful. He even fell down and threw up in the hall. Of course he wasn't as dirty as Lisa's father. But she can't help that he's like that. I like her," she finished slowly.

"I wasn't so much scared as I was sorry for Lisa," Ann put in. "She looked as though she felt so bad about it. I suppose they hadn't expected him home and didn't think we'd see him like that. You can tell she loves her father."

They didn't say much more on the way home. Peggy had a queer feeling as she realized this was her last night in California. It didn't seem real that in just a few days this would all be something in the past.

"Dad will be here early." Ann yawned into the silence as they walked up the steps and into the house. "I suppose we'd better get to bed right away."

"I suppose so," Peggy answered regretfully. "But I'm too excited to sleep."

As they started up the stairs, Aunt Emily spoke from behind them. "Peggy, perhaps we had better say good-bye, tonight. Would you come in here a minute?"

"Yes, Aunt Emily," Peggy answered meekly and crossed the hall toward her. Ann and Jane went on upstairs while Peggy trailed behind her aunt into the living room.

"Sit down a moment, Peggy. I shan't keep you long."

Peggy sat down mutely, wishing that this last interview were over but being glad it was the last.

"I trust you will not have too many unpleasant memories of your stay here, my dear. I must say I was rather reluctant to take on the responsibility when your mother first approached me about the possibility of your visit. I think had I known it would last for the entire year, I might not have agreed. but we have managed, and I think you have benefited in many ways."

It was not a question but a statement, and Peggy felt obligated to nod agreement, though her aunt's manner infuriated her.

"I hope Jane will not have been too unsettled by the visit, though perhaps she may miss your company for a few days." She rose abruptly. "Have a good trip. We'll be glad to hear from you now and then if you should care to write."

At that moment Peggy wanted to run and unpack every single thing her aunt had given her and dump them at her feet. But she made herself smile and say distantly, "Thank you for everything you gave me. It was nice of you."

"You are welcome. Run along now."

As soon as she left the living room and her aunt's presence, Peggy did run and burst furiously into her bedroom, slamming the door behind her.

"Honestly, she makes me so mad I could cry!"

"What's the matter?" Ann looked out from the bathroom questioningly and spoke through the foam of toothpaste. "What'd she say?"

"It isn't really what she *said.* All she did was say good-bye. But she makes it sound as though I were some—some *thing* that it was her duty to make something of. though she doubts that she has succeeded."

"I feel sorry for her."

"For Aunt Emily? Don't waste your time!"

Ann didn't answer as Peggy yanked off her dress and thrust it into the open suitcase on her bed. But Ann's words seemed to echo in the room as Peggy finished getting ready for bed, moved her suitcase off, and climbed in.

"Oh, I suppose you're right!" she finally admitted. "I know you are. But you haven't had to live with her."

"I know this will sound preachy—" Ann laughed. "It should, I guess, because it comes from a preacher. My folks always tell me there's a reason people are the way they are. Their background or family or training and experiences they've had. For instance, I don't get easily excited over things because my folks don't. You react in certain ways because that's the way you are. Your aunt is like that too."

"I suppose so," Peggy agreed. "I guess my main trouble is that I really don't want to feel sorry for her—or even like her."

Ann reached for her Bible, and after a moment Peggy reached for hers, too. For a little while the room was quiet as they both read and prayed. Peggy finished first and waited until Ann put her Bible down.

"I don't think I really meant what I said about my aunt."

"I know you didn't," Ann replied. "I know you well enough to know that you say things sometimes that you don't really mean. When you cool off a little, you admit you don't mean them either. Your aunt is probably like that in her way. Maybe she doesn't mean things to sound the way they do at all." Ann laughed. "Maybe you and she are more alike than you know."

"Ann!" Peggy's voice carried her anger and hurt. But in the silence, she sat up in bed abruptly and swung her legs over the side.

"I think you're right," she exclaimed, searching for her slippers. "I'm going downstairs and tell her how I really feel."

Ann sat up in alarm. "Are you sure you know what you're doing now?"

But Peggy flew out of the room without answering and down the stairs. Her footsteps were lost in the thick carpeting as she slipped swiftly through the darkened living room to Aunt Emily's study. The door was slightly ajar, and she could see her aunt standing at the window, her back to the room.

"Aunt Emily, I couldn't go away letting you think I didn't appreciate being able to live here. It was awfully nice of you to let me come and to do so much for me."

As she looked at her aunt's rigid back and unyielding shoulders, she began to regret the impulsive decision that had brought her down in such a hurry. Then her aunt turned, and Peggy saw with amazement the traces of tears on her cheeks.

But her voice was as controlled as ever as she replied, "Thank you for coming down like this, Peggy. Sometimes people misunderstand one another because they are afraid to express their emotions. I'm afraid this has been our trouble during the past year."

Peggy took a few quick steps forward, reached up, and kissed her aunt's cheek. Then she ran from the room and back upstairs.

"I'm glad I did it," she reported to Ann a few minutes later. "I think she's lonely in her way."

"And maybe a little bit afraid too," Ann said soberly. "I mean, afraid that things will be different now that your uncle is a Christian. She wouldn't know that that isn't anything to be afraid of."

Peggy sat up in bed and clasped her arms around her knees. "You know, it's funny how things turn out. I've thought all year that I was the one who would have to see to it that everybody here became a Christian. And it hasn't been that way at all," she admitted soberly. "In fact, if it had been left to me, nothing would have happened. I did help Lisa a little, but I didn't have a thing to do with Uncle Walter's being saved. It was Mr. Ferguson who helped him."

Ann nodded. "And now your uncle can help your aunt, and maybe Lisa will be the one to show Jane what it means to be a Christian. There's no telling what might happen out here in the next few months. It's kind of exciting to think about, isn't it?"

Peggy settled back on her pillow and reached to snap off the bed lamp. "Honestly, Ann, I hope I've learned a lesson! From now on I'm going to look for the nice things to happen instead of expecting the worst all the time. And the very *nicest* is that I'm going home!"